Laurence Green is a ghostwriter, novelist, poet, and biographer. He began writing after retiring from teaching; and enjoys living in the small Devon village he has lived in since the age of five. He is a historian, with a particular interest in the Great War and the American Civil War. Happily married for over fifty years, he enjoys travelling, gardening and dry stone walling; the poetry of Charles Causley and the music of George Butterworth. It took him seventy years before he saw his first ghost. He is a churchwarden and Street Pastor.

Antonio Monteiro and Maeve Vickery.

Laurence Green

A HAUNTED PARISH

AUSTIN MACAULEY PUBLISHERS™
LONDON • CAMBRIDGE • NEW YORK • SHARJAH

Copyright © Laurence Green 2024

The right of Laurence Green to be identified as the author of this work has been asserted by the author in accordance with sections 77 and 78 of the Copyright, Designs and Patents Act 1988.

All rights reserved. No part of this publication may be reproduced, stored in a retrieval system, or transmitted in any form or by any means, electronic, mechanical, photocopying, recording, or otherwise, without the prior permission of the publishers.

Any person who commits any unauthorised act in relation to this publication may be liable to criminal prosecution and civil claims for damages.

This is a work of fiction. Names, characters, businesses, places, events, locales, and incidents are either the products of the author's imagination or used in a fictitious manner. Any resemblance to actual persons, living or dead, or actual events is purely coincidental.

A CIP catalogue record for this title is available from the British Library.

ISBN 9781035899920 (Paperback)
ISBN 9781035832194 (ePub e-book)

www.austinmacauley.co.uk

First Published 2024
Austin Macauley Publishers Ltd®
1 Canada Square
Canary Wharf
London
E14 5AA

I would like to thank A Ghostly Company for their encouragement and help as well as all my previous publishers: Moorhen, Fighting High, Cornovia Press, and Scryfa. Thank you to Catharine Collingridge for the cover illustration and my wife, Kathi, for help with the computer.

Wind in the Pipes

Nearly everyone was pleased when the new Team Rector was appointed to the North Cornwall Team Ministry. The interregnum had been long and difficult; retired vicars had struggled to take the services at the three far-flung parishes that made up the team. Loosely linked together by poor church finances, dodgy geography and the whim of the archdeacon, the sparsely populated parishes clung either to rocky cliffs above the long Atlantic rollers or to the thin soils of wind-blasted uplands further inland. Roughly in the middle lay the parish of Goonperran where the ancient granite church crouched behind bent trees and thorn hedges in the middle of the village.

The Reverend Tim Tremaine came from down west in Cornwall. Dragged up on a council estate in Penzance, he was no stranger to deprivation and danger. After leaving school with a handful of GCSEs, he joined the army and, putting his bad ways behind him, quickly rose to the rank of staff sergeant in the Royal Wessex Rifles. His tours of Iraq and Afghanistan were marked by violent deaths by IEDs, small arms fire and enemy rockets. He emerged mostly unscathed; his wounds had been mostly physical.

In his late twenties, he put himself into theological college, surprised himself by how much he liked it and gained a good theological degree. After a turbulent three-year curacy in Plymouth, he applied for the scattered North Cornish parishes. He never kidded himself that his life would become easy. He needed a new and completely different set of challenges and make no mistake my 'andsomes, there were plenty where he was going.

His interview took place in Goonperran Village Hall before six churchwardens, the archdeacon, and the patron of the living, Lord Carlyon. Tim liked nearly all of the interviewers. The churchwardens were a mixture of farmers, young men of indeterminate profession, and a couple of retired incomers. One of the young men wore the bleached and tangled hair of a surfer. Tim warmed to that.

He wasn't the only candidate for the post. One other, older, man from Surrey was obviously there for an easement into retirement. He didn't stand a chance, and Tim was offered the job. With only a short pause, he accepted.

The Vicarage was small and sparse, with thick granite walls and small windows. It squatted next to the church of St Piran under a shelter belt of beech trees. It had a small garden and a shed that Tim could use as a workshop. He liked it. So did his fiancée Elizabeth when she came up from Truro to see it. Tim busily installed his books on the rickety shelves in his study. Rooks cawed in the bare trees outside as winter arrived from up country.

Tim made sure to visit all his parishes and made contact with as many people as he could. He was amused by their reaction to his battered old car, a dented Volkswagen Golf. Many of the locals looked at it with approval; many of the incomers looked down their noses at it. When they saw the bumper sticker, which stated 'My Boss is a Jewish Carpenter', his disapproval rating went up in certain areas with second homes.

His life soon fell into a routine, one that he loved. Apart from taking services, endless meetings, unfathomable admin, and visits, he walked over to St Piran's to say the daily offices. He never found this a chore and looked forward to being alone in the church with God. His prayer life developed incrementally during his early days in the three parishes.

One chilly evening as the sun was sinking down in a fiery orb at just after four o'clock, Tim wrapped himself in his heavy burial cloak and set off to say evensong in the unheated church. He was pondering what to do about the organist at St Piran's who was showing signs of advanced dementia, sometimes forgetting to take off her gloves before playing completely the wrong hymn tune.

As Tim turned the handle of the church door, he felt uneasy. The atmosphere of the building had subtly changed. It was even colder than usual. Had someone left the windows open? A quick glance at the flaps in the Victorian stained glass windows showed them all firmly closed. Tim felt as if he were being watched.

The place was icy cold, his breath rose in plumes unseen since his youthful experiments with cannabis. He crossed himself before kneeling at the altar rail and beginning the prayers for evensong. He was aware of the darkening windows surrounding him and the echoes reverberating around the nave and the aisles each time he moved his shoe against the granite slab of the floor.

Then he heard it, a rushing sound like a mighty wind, from the organ. A few quiet random notes followed, curiously muted. Then, as if from a far distance, Boellmann's *Toccata* crashed against his ears. Tim stood up, put down his prayer book, and turned round to look over the choir stalls at the organ. Realising that it couldn't have been Mrs Penberthy practising for Sunday, he was puzzled by the intrusion. Indeed he had never heard Mrs P play anything more challenging than a faltering *'O for the wings of a dove'*.

Tim could see that someone was playing the organ and playing it very well. He could just make out a hunched figure swaying with the wild rhythm of the music, his feet pumping the pedals, his hands pulling out and pushing in the stops. Tim didn't want to interrupt the playing while feeling strange and slightly put out that his evensong had been disturbed. He looked away at the west window bathed in the fading reds of the setting sun.

When he looked back the organ bench was empty as the organ continued to play. Tim could see the white and black keys depressed, the pedals rise and fall, and the stops going in and out. The piece came to its frantic climax. The final notes echoed around the cold church as Tim heard the organ pump switched off and the wooden cover pulled down over the keys. Then all was quiet, as silent as a tomb.

With a huge effort of will, Tim knelt down and finished the office of evensong. He stood up, crossed himself and walked out of the echoing church, switching off the lights and locking the ancient oak door with a heavy iron key. Back in the warmth of the Vicarage, he pondered what had happened. Someone could have played a trick on him by playing the organ music from an instrument under one of the windows.

They could have projected an animated figure through a window opposite the organ. But how would that account for the movement of keys, pedals and stops? Why would someone go to all the trouble of setting up an elaborate hoax in a dim and frosty churchyard when the Carlyon Arms was open with a log fire and real ale?

That night Tim prayed about what he had experienced. Surely he couldn't be suffering from overwork when he was only weeks into his new ministry. He was enjoying the challenges of getting to know each parish and any problems he was encountering were minor. One of them, of course, was what to do about the organist Mrs Penberthy.

Was he suffering from Post Traumatic Stress Syndrome? Had his sometimes horrific experiences in hot and alien lands come home to roost? He didn't think so. He occasionally dreamed about foot patrols down dusty streets, encounters with snipers, and IEDs going off, but that was perfectly normal. Perhaps this manifestation was objective and trying to tell him something.

As the weeks went by and winter softened into the wet Cornish spring that Tim remembered from long ago the involuntary organ recitals became more frequent. They were invariably accompanied by a sudden drop in temperature and feelings of gloom and even, sometimes, of depression. Tim decided to talk to his two churchwardens in his study.

George Ould and Patricia Thomson were both good and faithful people. George had farmed in the parish and then, unusual for Cornwall, handed the whole farm over to his son and his son's wife, saying to all and sundry; "I wasn't born to work until I drop." Patricia had moved into the parish with her husband when he had taken early retirement as headmaster of a large secondary school in Bude. Tim liked and trusted them both.

All three sat in comfortable chairs in the Vicarage study, a good cup of coffee in their hands.

George began first: "I can tell what this is about, Rector. I can tell by how you look. It's been going on for years and had driven more vicars away than I can remember. We didn't bring it up during the interview because you'd have thought us mazed in the head. We also thought that it might not happen to you. Not very honest of us and we apologise. But here we are. T'idden wind in the pipes neither. 'Tis Brian, our wonderful organist, who died many years ago.

"You haven't had a nervous breakdown like Mr Rudall or run off like Mr Cave. You'm still here and we want to keep you. We'll do what we can to help you, you can depend on that."

Tim replied, "Thank you for that, George. I don't feel that anyone acted wrongly over this matter. Perhaps I've been sent here to do something about it. I've been praying about it and shall seek advice from the Diocesan Deliverance Officer."

"I didn't know we had one," said Patricia. "Does this mean a service of exorcism for poor old Brian?"

"Certainly not," replied Tim. "Exorcism is used to send evil spirits, demons if you like, to God to sort out. We don't send souls to hell either these days. Deliverance is a much gentler process even though we must be on our guard not to let evil spirits in on the act through any weakness or occasion of sin on our part. Deliverance exists to direct lost souls towards God and show them where to find the light. Exorcism is only for dealing with demons."

"Strong stuff," said George. "We certainly need help and advice."

"Tell me about Brian, please."

Patricia sat back in her chair.

"Brian Paterson was a very good organist indeed. He had studied at the Royal College of Music and was a professional. He had even made recordings on vinyl. He came here during the fifties to retire with his wife after a long and distinguished career. A few years after they moved here his wife Mavis fell down Penjawler Cliff onto Porthpedner Beach. She survived the fall but fell into a decline and died a few weeks later.

"Brian was devastated and fell into depression. The trouble is that nobody knew it. It was a great shock when his body was found on Porthpedner Beach one Sunday afternoon after he had played the organ for the morning service at St Piran's. People still remember his playing Boellmann's *Toccata* at the end of the service with great gusto.

"Although no note was found suicide was presumed. The coroner ruled that it was suicide and poor Brian couldn't have a proper funeral service and was buried in unconsecrated ground in the new village cemetery.

"While Brian's body lay in the hearse outside the church the first part of the funeral service was said for him. Back then the church didn't allow the committal for suicides, so Brian went to his grave without the benefit of a full and proper funeral. I think I've got it right; I wasn't here back in the fifties."

"It's all right and proper, just as you told it," said George. "I remember Brian very well. Between these four walls, we've never had such a good organist before, nor since. He trained the choir to sing just beautifully. If he did top himself, I can't find it in me to blame him."

"I'm very glad to say that the Church doesn't judge people like it used to. We must find a way to help Brian to find his way back to God."

That night, Tim had a very vivid dream. He was walking on top of a high cliff looking down on a wide beach with jagged rocks protruding. The sun cast long rays over the waves that seemed to roll in from Newfoundland. A lone figure stood on the cliff's edge looking out to sea with a bunch of flowers in his hand. Behind him was a dark cloud that seemed to throb with malice.

As it swirled around, a menacing figure could be made out writhing within it. As Brian swung his arm back to throw the flowers onto the beach, the cloud enveloped him, and the cliff edge crumbled and gave way. The man went over with a quantity of earth, stones and turf. Tim ran to where he had gone over, hoping to find him on a ledge not far down the cliff. But he saw the sprawled, tiny figure broken on the rocks below. Tim felt himself shouting 'Brian' just before he woke up.

The dream had ended but someone stood at the foot of Tim's bed, an indistinct shape with the head at an odd angle and one arm impossibly bent. A voice came into Tim's head: 'That's what happened to me on Penjawler Cliff. My death, although welcome, was mainly accidental.'

Next morning, Tim made an appointment with the deliverance officer and the bishop in Truro. The three clerics were to meet later in the week in the bishop's office. Then Tim went to visit Mrs Penberthy in her small grey house at the end of the village.

"Come in," she responded to the doorbell's soft ring. "Good to see you, Rector. I feel that I owe you an explanation."

She ushered him into a snug living room and sat him down in an armchair.

"'Tis like this, Rector. I'm not as young as I was but I definitely don't have the dementia." She pointed to the completed crossword of today's Western Morning News. "I don't know why my organ playing has gone off. It is as if someone is sitting on the bench beside me and putting his hands over mine at times. It depresses me and I feel exhausted just by being there. I don't know whether to carry on or chuck it in, I really don't."

"What you've told me is very important. I think we are being interfered with. Are you aware of the history of Brian Paterson?"

"Yes, I am, but I never met Mr Paterson. He was before my time. When he was here, I was starting work at Illogan Library. Do you think he comes back?"

She sounded so matter-of-fact that Tim felt a slight shudder in his back.

"Yes, I think he does. He means no harm but is lost, unable to find his way back to the light and to God. I think it's time we helped him to do that. Please don't stop being our organist. We need you there, all of us need you there at the organ where you belong."

"'Tis nice of you to put it like that. I'd love to stay on if I can play well enough."

"I'm going to see the bishop at the end of the week to see how we can send Brian to his rest. Please play the organ for us on Sunday as usual."

On his way home, Tim wondered if he was doing the right thing by exposing Mrs P to another possible psychic undermining. He would pray about it.

Friday was a bright and breezy day as Tim drove to Truro. He realised that it was the first time he had been out of the parishes since he had moved into the Vicarage in Goonperran. He was determined to enjoy this brief outing. Approaching Truro he saw the three spires of Pearson's magnificent Victorian cathedral with their Breton lanterns. He managed to park not far from the bishop's office and walked across the granite cobbles in the sunshine.

He was surprised at the plainness and austerity of the office with its unadorned walls and stark crucifix. The bishop asked him to sit down and folded his hands across his chest. He was in no hurry and prepared to listen. His face twinkled with amusement.

"You don't have to call me sir, Tim. You're not in the army now. Call me Gerald."

"Thank you, Gerald. Old habits die hard. I've come about a haunting..." He told the bishop about what he had heard and seen and how he proposed to tackle the problem. The bishop leaned forward with intense interest.

"In a few minutes, Frank will be here. He's the Diocesan Deliverance Officer. We don't broadcast this for obvious reasons. It is a vital part of our mission to direct lost souls to God. We have to be careful of two things: the press and the devil. The latter can worm his way in a similar manner to the former. We must be constantly on our guard against Satan taking advantage of any weakness or confusion in deliverance."

There was a sharp rap on the door and a tall, elderly parson came in and sat down, perfectly at home with the bishop and anyone else in the room. After introductions, Tim told the story again.

Frank looked thoughtful.

"I'm surprised that this one hasn't popped up before. It's been going on for a long time and seems to be growing stronger, probably because of a new rector in the parish. It could be more than a cry for help. There is a real risk of possession here so we must proceed with care.

"I suggest a brief Deliverance during the service on Sunday. The Church will be acting as a whole body and I strongly advocate a period of prayer and fasting before the service. I will be there for it and will arrive at the end of the communion just before the Deliverance."

"Thank you, Frank. I need your permission, Gerald, to do this. I am determined that it will succeed."

"You have my unreserved permission and blessing. May God be with you."

When Tim had left the office Frank turned to Gerald and said: "I have a feeling that this will be a tough one…"

On Saturday, Tim shut himself in his study, cancelled all appointments, and prayed and fasted. He drank only water and ate a few dry biscuits. He went to bed early after a long talk on the phone with Elizabeth, his fiancée.

The dream came back once with startling clarity. This time it was slightly different. As Tim stood at the cliff's edge at Penjawler admiring the sun's rays slanting across the ocean he noticed two figures to his left uphill from him. One held a bunch of flowers; the other crept up behind him. There was no fog this time but the feeling of menace was all-pervading.

As Brian's arm went back to throw the flowers the dark figure behind him leapt forward and pushed him off the edge. At the same time, the cliff edge crumbled and the assailant vanished. As before Tim ran up to the top and looked over to see the sprawled figure far below, he woke up with a start and knelt down to pray.

The tinkly bells rang as usual in the high grey tower for Sunday church. The members of the congregation walked briskly up the church path in the east wind past slanting slate gravestones and tilting table tombs. They took their places as usual: the churchwardens beside their wands of office, the rest where they were most comfortable. Those with hearing loss sat at the front of the church and did not hide behind the squat granite pillars.

Tim walked steadily out of the vestry and waited a moment for Mrs P to finish the introit voluntarily. He thanked her and asked everyone to sit down. He told them that, at the service's end, he was going to perform a Deliverance, not an exorcism, for the repose of the soul of Brian Paterson, a former organist. He explained what he would do and why and finished by saying that he would pause at the end of the service for anyone to leave at that point.

The service went well but Mrs P was obviously struggling more than usual at the organ. Tim offered a silent prayer for her. His sermon consisted of explaining Deliverance, referring back to passages from the New Testament. At the end of the service a few people, mostly mothers with young children, got up to leave.

Tim went over to the choir stalls where a bowl of holy water and a sprig of box sat next to the organ. Where on earth was Frank, on whom he depended for strength and support? Did he, the Rector, have the faith and strength to carry out this ghost laying alone?

Sweating profusely he began the service of Deliverance and sprinkled the organ console and Mrs P with holy water.

So far so good... There was a collective gasp from the congregation as the south door opened and slammed shut and the temperature in the church dropped like a stone. A sound like the buzzing of angry wasps came from the screen near the organ.

Mrs Penberthy climbed rapidly off the organ bench and sat down at the back of the church as a cloud of vapour rose from the mouths of the priest and people. Then, with a harsh rumble, the organ began to play. The *Ave Maria* rose in pitch, badly and stumblingly played. It sounded wrong, cynical. Tim began to think of all the terrible things he had done before becoming a priest: the donkey he had shot in Iraq, the women he had betrayed, the men he had belittled. He gasped and dropped the prayer book as he realised who was now playing the organ. The demon had replaced Brian Paterson on the organ bench. Tim felt control slipping from him and began to feel faint. His breath came in short wheezes from a tightened chest. The nave of the church began to swim before his eyes as the insistent buzzing sound hurt his ears and made his head acutely ache.

The south door banged open again and Frank came hurriedly in. He stood at the crossing and said in a loud and ringing voice: "God has forgiven you your sins. Proceed in the strength of the Lord."

Tim picked up the book and took a deep breath. The faintness subsided and the buzzing became fainter. He rose up and shouted: "Be gone from here to the presence of the Almighty. Release your hold on Brian and never return here. In the name of Christ, be gone!"

The buzzing lost intensity as Tim and Frank continued to silently pray. Both men felt as if they had completed several rounds of Cornish wrestling. The organ stopped with a final tortured wheeze and the temperature rose in the church. Everyone was on their knees praying.

Tim then prayed in a loud voice for the soul of Brian Paterson. He commended Brian's soul to God and thanked Him for the reluctant departure of the demon.

Then Tim nodded to Mrs Penberthy who stood up and walked back to the organ. She sat down on the bench and pulled out some sheets of music. Flexing her fingers she began to play Boellmann's *Homage a la Sainte Vierge.* The notes rose and fell beautifully, and the piece was superbly played. At the end, the congregation clapped before rising from the benches and walking outside into the spring sunshine.

"Well done, Tim," said Frank. "You did it. Brian is now at rest and the demon that had taken over is banished. We must keep up our prayers to keep it that way."

"Thank you, Frank, for your prompt intervention. I don't think I could have continued on my own."

"It nearly didn't happen. All sorts of obstacles were put in my way to make me late: herds of cows and pigs, a flat tyre and an empty fuel tank."

"But why was Brian pushed down the cliff by a demon? He seems to have been a good man with no guilty secrets."

"He was in the wrong place at the wrong time. Penjawler Cliff is a well-known suicide spot like Beachy Head up country. 'Penjawler' is, in Cornish, the Devil's Headland, an accursed place from some evil deeds centuries ago. It seems to be a 'thin spot' dominated by the evil that has never gone away and feeds on grief and weakness. Remember that Satan prowls around seeking whom he may devour."

"Thank you for your advice and help, Frank. I have the feeling I might need your help again soon. In the meantime, I'll ask Mrs P to play the *Toccata* next week. I think she can do it on her own…"

Mother Knows Best

The day's work was nearly over. Rev. Tim had visited several parishioners, said the daily offices in the church, chaired a tedious meeting, fixed the lock on the church door and done a myriad of other everyday tasks before shutting himself in his study and picking up the phone. He talked for over half an hour to his fiancée Elizabeth in Truro before feeding the cat and starting to prepare supper for one.

His phone rang with an irritating urgency. He picked it up to learn that one of his parishioners had a problem. George Pumphrey had just come out of Treliske after a hernia operation on the condition that someone slept in his house the first night he was at home. His friend Ernie had just come down with flu and had to call off his night in George's house at the last moment. Could the vicar come and spend the night instead?

Of course, he could, thought Tim. But he didn't relish the prospect. George's tiny cottage was a run-down shrine to his late mother. Crumbling plaster, peeling wallpaper, patches of damp and dust everywhere covered shabby brown furniture and ruptured armchairs. Tim had visited there a few times and had enjoyed George's company but not the state of the house. It reminded him too clearly how the vicarage could become if he didn't take the time to do more housework.

George was a bachelor with a chequered past, like the curate's egg 'good in parts'. He had knocked around the world crewing yachts and had smuggled, struggled and snuggled. Tim didn't really want to know the details. Life had left its mark on George; scars ran down his face and arms. But he was good company and could talk about fascinating experiences, fascinating if you hadn't heard them more than once. He was in his late seventies and as strong as an ox. His wild grey hair tumbled over his forehead giving him a bohemian air.

After unspeakable voyages under mad skippers, he settled down to build boats and maintain them. As he grew older, he ended up running the stores and then came home to look after his ailing mother.

She was a formidable woman. When her husband found out that she was suffering from rheumatoid arthritis, he took himself over to the fleshpots of Spain, never to return. She brought George up strictly and well. George had enough of his father in him to be mildly disreputable and enough of his mother to be dutiful and caring.

Eventually, Alice died after turning her invalid carriage over one last time. George inherited the house but did nothing to it. Tim found himself thinking of Miss Havisham as he dug out the old army sleeping bag that he should have handed in on leaving the army. Render unto Caesar, etc.

Saying goodnight to Crowley the cat, Tim let himself out of the vicarage. It was a warm summer night twinkling with distant stars. Owls hooted from the ring of tall trees that encircled the churchyard. Tim carried his overnight bag past the lych-gate and followed the granite wall around to the lane where George's cottage was.

He knocked on the rough door and heard shuffling footsteps as George came to let him in.

"Good of you to come, Vicar," he said as he bent over to relieve the pain of the operation. "Your room's at the head of the stairs. I hope you'll be comfortable. The bed's less than twenty years old."

"I'll turn in now George if you don't mind. I've had a busy day and tomorrow promises to be the same. Sleep well. I won't disturb you, but if you have a problem during the night, just call out and I'll be with you. May God bless you and give you a restful night."

And me too, he thought as he climbed the steep, worn stairs to his dusty bedroom. Before unrolling his sleeping bag onto the divan bed, Tim found the bathroom and washed and brushed his teeth. He was amused to see that the toilet had a tank and chain up by the sagging ceiling. It was probably the only one left in the parish.

Before turning in, Tim listened at George's door. A soft snore reassured him that George was safely asleep and would probably remain so. Then Tim said his prayers before unzipping his bag and lying down. It's funny how army sleeping bags always retained the smell of mould however much you aired them.

Three loud bangs on the front door interrupted Tim's dream of leading a patrol of Wolf Cubs up a dusty lane in

Helmand. He struggled out of the malodorous sleeping bag and crept down the stairs to the hallway. He cautiously opened the front door to find no one there. Shivering in the pre-dawn chill, he closed the door and walked into a cloud of freezing air at the bottom of the stairs. With a huge effort of will, he pushed through it and ran lightly up the splintery stairs. Feeling incredibly tired, he climbed back into his warm sleeping bag and was settling down to sleep when he heard a sharp tapping from the stairs.

Cursing silently because he didn't want George disturbed, he quietly reopened his bedroom door. Near the bottom of the staircase and just around the bend was a faint cloud of cold light that seemed to grow brighter as it advanced up the stairs. The tapping had stopped.

Tim's mouth fell open as a misty figure appeared to be gliding up the stairs. He could see the top of its head with grey, sparse hair straggling over the ears. The face turned up to Tim. It was pale and rigid with glaring eyes, deeply lined and without expression. But what was infinitely worse was the legs. They were rigid and unbending, supported by two hospital crutches. Swollen bandaged feet stuck out at an angle as the apparition glided up the stairs towards him.

Tim felt all will and energy drain out of him. He could only watch as the dreadful figure drew up to him. The sightless eyes bored through him with no sign of recognition. Tim was able to cross himself as the spectre vanished through the door of George's room. He staggered back into his own room to collapse onto his bed before passing out.

Early in the morning, Tim woke up from a deep sleep, much refreshed despite what he considered was a bad nightmare. He dressed and listened at George's door. All was quiet so he opened the door with a cheery, "Good morning, George."

Then he saw that George was in no state to reply. He lay on his back with a faint smile on his face looking peaceful and calm. One arm lay on the eiderdown, but George was dead.

Tim immediately rang for an ambulance and said some prayers for the repose of George's soul. He now knew who the old woman had been and why she had visited in the middle of the night. Despite her sinister appearance, she had been benign. She had come to welcome her son home, not to kill him but to ease his passing.

Later in the day, after the paramedics had removed George's stiff remains, Tim sat in his office in the vicarage and tried to find out if George had any relatives or close friends. The results of his enquiries were negative so Tim phoned George's solicitor, whose name he had found on a dusty shelf in the cottage. George had left a will, which would soon be read. Would Tim mind being present when it was?

A few days later, the coroner released George's body with the finding that George had died in his sleep of heart failure and that no foul play was suspected. Tim and the solicitor, Mr Barnes of Barnes and Clemo, arranged the funeral for the following Saturday at St Piran's Church. After the committal, George was to be cremated, and his ashes placed with those of his mother in the churchyard.

The day of the funeral was sunny and breezy. Tim was surprised by how many of the villagers were there to send George on his way. He preached on 'Who is my Neighbour?' to a silent congregation, many of whom really had little time for George. Just before the end of the sermon, Tim noticed a grey-haired old lady sitting at the back of the nave on her own. Her two crutches rested on the bench in front as she looked at him with a faint smile.

After the committal, Tim saw the lady stand slowly up and walk silently out of the church, leaving her crutches behind. She did not appear to move stiffly, and with a smile and a faint wave of the hand, she vanished through the massive oaken west door.

At the service's conclusion, Tim accompanied the coffin out to the hearse and prepared to drive to Bodmin Crematorium. But, first, he felt compelled to clear away the crutches from the bench at the back of the nave. He wasn't surprised that they were no longer there, only a couple of scratches to indicate where they had hooked onto the back of the bench in front.

Two weeks later, Tim was summoned to the offices of Barnes and Clemo, Solicitors and Notaries Public. Mr Barnes sat him down with a cup of tea and warned him that the will could prove controversial. Tim learned that George had left his cottage and what money he had to him, The Reverend Tim Tremaine. The reason that the will was potentially controversial was that Tim had been in the house when George had died, thus providing opportunity as well as motive. No one was exempt from the law of suspicion.

The following Tuesday, the Parochial Church Council met in Tim's cramped office in the vicarage. Tim said the opening prayer and then launched straight into what was on his mind.

"I'm sure you all know by now that George, for reasons of his own, left his house and remaining money to me. You can imagine how surprised I was when I found out and how quickly I realised the position his decision had put me in. With God's help, I have reached a decision concerning what I will do with the house and the money. I want it all to go to St Piran's.

"There are two options open to us: either we keep the house and restore it to provide an affordable home at an affordable rent to a local family or we sell it and spend the money on re-ordering the church. The decision is yours. I shall abide by what you decide. Take your time over it and let me know."

The youngest person on the PCC, Jowan Hoskin, spoke up.

"I vote we keep the house and rent it out. There are plenty of local families struggling to rent properties in this parish from second homeowners from up country. Let's voluntarily do the place up and let it at an affordable rent!"

The rest of the council agreed wholeheartedly, and it was put to the vote. The decision was unanimous, and for once, the council felt it had achieved something. Mr Warren, a farmer and the oldest member of the council summed it up in a few words:

"That's how it belongs to be..."

Sworn Innocence

One windy autumn morning, Rev. Tim decided to pop round to George Pumphrey's old house to see how the restoration work was going. He pulled on his old camo jacket (which he should have handed in on leaving the army) and set out around the churchyard wall. The wind tugged at his ragged jeans and threatened to spring loose his clerical collar. Elizabeth was always reminding him that he was scruffy, needing a shave or a haircut. But she did it nicely, and sometimes, Tim found time to tidy himself up. Today, as usual, was an exception.

Rounding a windy corner Tim saw the cottage ahead of him. It looked very different from the night George had died. The roof had been mended; the windows scraped and painted; and the front door rubbed down and painted green. All this work had been done by volunteers in the parish, many of them not church attenders. Hammering and sawing were audible and the old echoing clatter and cursing too.

Tim knocked at the door and walked into the smell of fresh paint and newly sawn wood. Three men and a woman were hard at work stripping mouldy wallpaper and sanding dented wood. The woman was sawing planks to repair the floor.

"Bugger!" yelled young Hoskin as he dropped a hammer on his foot for the third time that day. "Oh, sorry, Vicar."

"Do you think I never bleddy swear sometimes?" replied Tim with a grin.

"But there's a woman here..." replied Jowan Hoskin. "'Tiddn't right."

"Balls!" retorted Lucy Tremlett. "It gets the bleddy job done."

The house was coming on well. All the labour had been voluntary, and most of the materials were donated or scrounged. Even the electricians and roofers had donated their time and skill.

The phone in Tim's pocket shrilled a Hail Mary. He groped for it and managed to answer it before the ringtone stopped. The bishop's secretary was ringing him. She sounded serious.

"The bishop would like to see you in his office at nine o'clock tomorrow morning. Please treat this with the utmost seriousness and be there. Goodbye."

Tim wondered why the secretary sounded so brusque and disapproving. Well, he would find out tomorrow. Sufficient unto the day is the evil thereof. The joy had gone out of the day, and Tim excused himself after thanking them for their hard work and skill. He decided to visit some of the older and sicker parishioners to take his mind off the meeting with the bishop.

Next morning, he shaved and put on clean clothes. He was at the bishop's office wondering what on earth the meeting could be about. The secretary, normally so bright and friendly, looked at him sideways as she ushered him into the bishop's office.

"Sit down, Tim," said the bishop gravely. "There have been some serious allegations against you in your parish. I want to hear what you have to say about them." He had not quite made up his mind yet but was looking dubious.

"I must admit that my language has been a bit salty just lately. I'm surprised that anyone would see fit to report it to you, however."

"It's something much more serious than that, Tim. Members of your choir say that you have been touching them inappropriately and even fondling them. Men and women have both brought this up. Apparently, it happened last Thursday after choir practice in the churchyard."

"But, sir, Gerald, I wasn't at choir practice last Thursday. I was giving the last rites to Mrs Uren at Halinnick Farm. How could I have possibly done such a thing? I am always very careful about touching people. In the army, we had a no-touching rule which was strictly enforced. I often had to remind young squaddies to leave female soldiers alone before they were knocked down."

"Tell me honestly, Tim. Has anything inappropriate ever happened between you and any of your parishioners, even in fun?"

"Never, I swear. It is a weakness I'm aware of and so take steps never to succumb to it. I would never tell you a lie, and I'll try to get to find out just what really happened. Please believe me. I wouldn't add a lie to my list of sins and weaknesses."

"I want to believe you Tim, but it's difficult. Surely, members of your choir who know you well couldn't fail to recognise you."

"I can't explain it, Gerald. But I'm determined to get to the truth of this."

He nearly said, "Get to the bottom of this," but stopped himself just in time.

The two men parted on good terms. The bishop, however, was determined to dismiss Tim if he were to be found guilty of this foolish action. He could not be seen to do nothing in such a serious safeguarding issue.

Tim slept badly that night. In his dreams, he returned to drunken encounters with the women of his youth. But he knew that he had never treated anyone in his parish with anything but the utmost respect. He felt soiled, raw, and vulnerable. When he woke up, he went to shave in the bathroom, glancing into the misty bathroom mirror before lathering his face.

He saw his face looking back at him and behind, and just to the left, another identical face.

There must have been something wrong with the mirror, Tim thought as he rubbed the condensation away. But no, there were two identical faces, one behind the other. Both had the same stubble and the same expression until the face at the back began to change. A cynical grin spread across the lower part of the face and the left eye closed in a lewd wink.

Tim cried out in surprise, hurriedly crossed himself and began to say the Lord's Prayer in a loud, strong voice. The image began to fade and soon disappeared entirely. Tim carried on shaving and prepared to go out.

After saying the office in church, Tim walked to George's cottage. He was disappointed to find it empty and locked up. No volunteers at work this morning; Tim thought he knew why. He saw very few people as he walked back through the village. Those he saw turned away, barely meeting his eye. The story was out.

Back in church, Tim knelt down at the altar rails and prayed. Then he sat in the choir stalls and thought. Before a solution could be found, he had to face what was really happening to him. He knew that he had, at no point, done anything wrong. But how could he convince his congregation, the village people, and the bishop that he was totally innocent? Most people knew of his chequered past; he had made no secret of it.

Then the truth came to him. Some diabolical agency was plotting his downfall, using the past to chip away at his self-confidence. Satan was a cunning fellow, a trick cyclist at the best of times. There had to be a solution.

There were, in fact, two solutions: Elizabeth and Frank. He would phone both of them immediately. The weekend was coming up, and Elizabeth would be free to come up and stay with him. Separate bedrooms (darn it!). Frank would also possibly have some time to see him.

Back in the vicarage, Tim dialled Elizabeth's number. She answered straight away.

"Elizabeth Penaluna."

"Hello, Liz, it's me. Can you come up here for the weekend? I have a problem, which you might be able to help me with. Please could you bring your camera?"

"Tim, you don't sound like yourself. Is everything alright? I'll come directly this evening. Whatever it is, we can talk about it. See you soon, love."

Next, Tim rang Frank.

"Frank, I really need your help. Could you come here tomorrow around 10:00 hours?"

"Of course, Tim. I'll be there, and we can talk about it. I think I know what it could be. I'll bring the bag."

"Thanks, Frank. I owe you. See you tomorrow. God bless you."

Tim stayed in the vicarage writing his sermon for Sunday. He doubted that there would be very many at church on Sunday now that the story had got out. He didn't blame the villagers. If he had done what he was accused of doing, he would have deserved to be shunned by everyone. He must remain strong in the knowledge that he had not done any of the sordid things he was accused of.

Early next morning, Elizabeth arrived in her ancient Renault. A primary school teacher's salary didn't stretch to affording a decent car. She was tall and slim, twenty-eight years old, with long dark hair. Like Tim, she spoke proper, with a Cornish accent.

She exuded common sense and sat quietly while Tim explained the situation. She trusted him totally and understood the problem.

"So you have a demon impersonating you, determined to bring you down and lay you low. That's really nasty. We can't let it happen. But who will believe you? People will think that you slipped back from Mrs Uren's in time to grope the choir in the churchyard. I know you would never have done that, but I know you much better than you do. What can we do?"

At that point the doorbell rank, and Frank let himself in with a cheery "'Ow, Be?" He sat down in the study and listened while Tim explained the situation once again. Unusually, the phone didn't ring at all during the course of that Saturday morning. Frank finally spoke:

"The demon thinks that it's in a position of strength; otherwise, it wouldn't have revealed itself in order to gloat. Pride will be its downfall. Satan's Achilles heel will always be arrogance and vanity. He is a self-publicist, a gloater. We shall make him fall into a trap of his own making."

"But how?" asked Elizabeth.

"We must expose his image so that he can be seen to be the deceiver and liar that he is."

"That's why you asked me to bring my camera?"

"That's right. I don't want to expose you to any danger, however."

"Given the life she has led up to now, I don't think Elizabeth is at any great risk. That might not be the case with you, Tim, so be on your guard. You must never doubt that you are a good priest and that any past transgressions are behind you. Just remember St Paul and the dreadful things he got up to before the road to Damascus."

Trapping a demon is not easy. He has to be outmanoeuvred, outthought and outprayed. As she walked around the village with Tim and Frank, Elizabeth took photographs of the two men. It was a long and frustrating business. By the end of the day, Tim was thoroughly demoralised and fed up. As they walked past the lych-gate for the seventh time, Tim stumbled and said out loud: "Oh, sod it," not caring who heard him. At that point, Liz took a rapid series of three photographs.

In the vicarage study, with the door firmly closed, the two priests and Elizabeth examined the day's pictures. The first twenty or thirty showed just two men walking around the village looking downcast. But the last three were something else.

The first showed Tim with his mouth open, Frank laughing, and a misty figure forming behind them in front of the lych-gate. The second showed Tim looking apologetic.

Frank continued to laugh, and the figure was now quite recognisably the double of Tim. The third showed the gloating expression on the figure's face as Tim and Frank turned to walk on.

"We have him," exclaimed Frank. "The camera never lies!"

"We need to show these photos to the bishop. If all three of us go to see him as soon as possible, we can convince him of the truth of Tim's innocence."

Fortunately, the bishop was free that evening and agreed to see Tim, Elizabeth, and Frank at Lys Escop. They drove down to Truro straight away and were ushered into the bishop's drawing room by his wife.

"Please sit down. I'm very glad you've come to see me. Frank, because you're here I think I know what this could be about. I've heard of doppelgangers before but need to see proof, you know. I have faith in all of you. With God's help, I will try to understand what has been happening in your parish."

Without saying a word, Tim handed the three prints of Elizabeth's photographs to the bishop. He looked at them for a long time.

"I want all three of you to swear that there has been no trickery here on your part, no Photoshop or digital manipulation of the images. Your whole future depends on your integrity and truthfulness."

All three looked the bishop in the eye and told him that the photos were exactly as taken. Finally, the bishop spoke again:

"I know that if Tim had been abusing members of the choir that Elizabeth would know it and have no tolerance for it. I am happy to see that she is still wearing her engagement ring. I know that Frank, a priest and deliverance consultant, would have no part in covering up such a thing. And I now know that Tim would never act disreputably either in or out of his parish. May God be praised!

"But now we must do two things: reassure the parish that Tim is not guilty and get rid of the demon that is determined to bring him down. I will cancel my appointments tomorrow and take the morning service at St Piran's. My sermon will be about not judging without knowing all the facts. Judge not that ye be not judged. Even if there are not many people in church tomorrow, the message will soon spread. I'll turn up early and walk about in the village."

"Thank you, Gerald, from the bottom of my heart."

"The second thing involves you, Frank. I'll give my permission for a Deliverance, or exorcism if necessary, to send this wicked demon back to God, or failing that, to outer darkness."

Next day, the Tenth Sunday after Trinity, many people arrived in church late, curious to know what the bishop was there for. Perhaps they expected an announcement that Tim was to be sacked. They had to wait for the sermon to find out.

"Satan roams around seeking whom he may devour. He sends demons to target men and women, to destroy their reputations and bring them down in the eyes of their friends and neighbours. He is cunning and totally unscrupulous, using lies and temptations to further his evil ends.

"This has happened to your vicar in this parish. It was a demon, believe it or not, who misbehaved in the churchyard, a form that resembled Tim in every respect while he was elsewhere. This is not just what I think. I have seen the evidence in the form of three photographs that clearly show a mocking image of Tim standing behind him outside this very church. It is an evil sight to look at. You will have to believe me, and I pray to God that you will do so.

"I put my reputation as your bishop on the line. Were I trying to cover up or push the affair under the carpet I would not be here asking for your trust and faith. Truth will out, and I have seen the proof. If any among you disbelieves me, I would ask them to talk to me after the service when I would show them the shocking truth."

After the service, a number of people came up to Tim and the bishop to thank them. They looked shocked and bemused, but they still had trust in the church. This had surely been a test of faith for everyone.

A few days later, Tim addressed the Parochial Church Council.

"Thank you for believing in the bishop and myself. I must apologise for seeming to bring bad influences into the parish. The Devil exploits weaknesses in us all. As you know my past life has not been exemplary and Satan is still trying to make me fail by inducing self-doubt and self-loathing. With your help and the help of all the village, he will not succeed.

"He is still out there plotting and subverting. But he is not intelligent. He only possesses low cunning."

"A bit like the Chairman of the Parish Council," muttered Hoskin. Tim glared at him in his best NCO manner before briefly smiling.

"You will see Frank and I doing what appear to be strange things outside the lych-gate this evening. Please keep well away for the time being. We will explain everything in due course when we're rid of the bugger, excuse me, beggar. Pray for us, we need all the strength we can summon. Thank you, all, and may God bless you and keep you from the Devil's wiles."

The red orb of the sun was sinking below the hills as Tim and Frank prepared for battle on the road in front of the lych-gate. Tim could imagine the howling of wolves but thought he had read too many gothic novels. Elizabeth and most of the congregation as well as a few villagers who never darkened the church doors were all shut in the church praying for Satan's banishment.

A huge black bat flitted along the road and circled the lych-gate. *Greater horseshoe*, Tim thought. He and Frank knelt on the dusty road in an attitude of prayer concentrating hard on summoning the demon. They knew that demons, like cats, are incurably curious and cannot resist being summoned.

This one was stubborn, however. An hour and a half after the prayers began a fog swirled around the lych-gate and materialised into Tim's double. It stood before the coffin slab watching with a slight smile on its face.

"I abjure you, son of Satan, to depart this place and never to return. Go straight into the light of God's presence and repent of your sins. Do not hesitate, but be gone now!"

The demon's form wavered and returned stronger than ever. It took a step forward towards the two men and raised its arms in a menacing way. It looked old, and its face gradually lost any resemblance to Tim. It was pure evil dressed in Tim's old clothes. It advanced by another step.

Both men held their ground. The demon was showing itself in its true form, trying to terrify them. Both men cried out in a loud voice:

"Begone, bastard son of Satan. You have no power to harm us here. Depart to outer darkness for eternity and leave the earth never to return. We command this in the name of God the Father, God the Son and God the Holy Spirit. Begone!"

Then, as both men intoned the Lord's Prayer, the demon took on a look of intense pain and frustration. It ground its teeth and howled before its outline began to waver. Flesh dissolved, and yellow bones showed through skin that was turning to parchment. With a loud shriek that shook the village, the demon was gone.

A loud cheer rose from the shadowy crowd in front of the Carlyon Arms. Clapping and cheers followed. A lone voice called out:

"There's a pint of Tinners' for each of you. Come and celebrate with us. We're glad to 'ave 'ee back!"

The church doors opened spilling light along the churchyard path. Elizabeth and the prayer group emerged to join the two priests at the pub. 'Thirst after righteousness...'

Private Spettigue

Rev Tim woke up in his comfortable bed with the spring sun streaming through his window. He rolled over luxuriating in the knowledge that he was on holiday for the next week. The weather was too nice to go anywhere else; Tim was determined to spend his time in Goonperran. He was mentally exhausted by his recent encounter with the doppelganger. Besides, he hadn't given himself the chance to sort out the vicarage garden. It was all brimbles and dyshuls; the flower beds infested with stroil and creeping ginny.

Tim wasn't fond of flower gardening, but he had grown up in a council house in Penzance where the whole back garden had been turned over to growing vegetables. He identified a patch of weedy lawn behind the vicarage and marked it out with binder cord for a vegetable patch. He took some old pallets that were leaning against the wall and tied them into a square compost frame. There was a Cornish shovel in the stone shed beside the house. The blade was rusty but the handle curved convincingly at the correct angle. There was even a rusty mattock that Tim determined to put to good use.

The gooks cawed in the high trees around the churchyard wall as Tim made a start. He even rolled up his sleeves, exposing an embarrassing tattoo of a nubile girl. Bending down, he grubbed off the turf from the rectangular plot he had marked out and laid the turves face down at the bottom of the compost frame. Smearing a bit of mud over his tattoo he leaned on his spade for a minute. Perhaps he would build a bench to sit on.

Several parishioners walking by said hello over the low granite wall of the vicarage. They seemed to approve of a vicar who got his hands dirty. Mrs Penberthy stopped to see how he was getting on as well as Mr Uren, the recently widowed farmer.

"Found anything yet, my 'andsome?" he called out.

"Only worms," Tim replied.

"Good sign."

As Tim bent down to begin the digging, he spotted a dome-shaped object that looked familiar. He bent down to pick it up and rubbed most of the earth off it. He could just make out the letters DCLI and a crown. That rang a bell; the Duke of Cornwall's Light Infantry had been the local regiment during the Great War. Doubtless men from the village had joined up and been sent away to France or Belgium. A number had never returned and lay either in Commonwealth War Cemeteries or under French or Belgian fields.

Straightening his back Tim left the garden, shut the gate and walked over to the War Memorial against the churchyard wall near the lych-gate. He read eight names of the fallen from World War I:

Private J Pascoe, DCLI
Corporal P Pascoe, DCLI
Private F W Wills, Royal Devon Yeomanry
Private W Uren, DCLI
Serjeant W Trenear, Devonshire regiment
Lieutenant J P S Posonby, DCLI
Private J D Spettigue MM, DCLI
Lance Bombardier W J Barnes, Royal Artillery.

There were three names from World War Two: two RAF and one Royal Navy.

Tim took the button to the pub at lunchtime and showed it to the locals in the bar. The landlord scratched his head; his family had only been in the village for two generations. An old man in a waistcoat took Tim to one side.

"They do say that a soldier who lived in your house before it became the vicarage was shot for cowardice in Belgium. I believe his name was Spettigue, but not the one on the memorial."

"So I suppose that he must have come home on leave before he went back to Ypres. He may have lost a button in the garden before he went back to the front."

"Strange family the Spettigues. They never got on for some reason. Cousins hated cousins. It was probably a quarrel over land or money or both. Jack Spettigue on the War Memorial was one of the good ones. His cousins were another matter."

"I must be getting along if I'm to finish half of my vegetable plot today. The weather could turn dirty tomorrow. Goodbye, Percy. Thanks for the information."

Tim went back to the garden and began digging. He turned the rich soil over, pulled up all the roots and left them to dry on the path. He worked up a rhythm, treading in the blade, raising and turning the rich soil without having to bend his back. The advantage of a Cornish spade was immense. You could also hold onto the shaft while bending down to pull weeds.

The blade had acquired a pleasing shine as the rust wore off. It slid in and out of the soil with ease. Soon Tim had found a 1918 penny, a horseshoe nail and a china doll's head. He put them carefully in a seed tray with the army button to clean up and display on a window sill.

Just before knocking off for tea, Tim spotted a curved piece of tarnished metal. He just missed damaging it with the sharp spade. Picking it up, he cleaned it by spitting on it. The letters DCLI emerged from the crust of the soil. Tim realised that it was a shoulder title, awarded to a soldier who had passed basic training during the Great War.

Had these bits of brass belonged to the soldier who was shot at dawn? Tim, with his interest in military history, intended to find out. He cleaned the spade and mattock and put them away in the shed. Then he went through the side door into the kitchen, made himself a cup of tea and fired up his battered laptop.

Under 'DCLI Shot at Dawn', he found a Private William Spettigue, 8th Battalion DCLI, shot for striking an officer at

Poperinge in July 1917. For this lapse of discipline and good manners, Spettigue was tried and sentenced to be shot at dawn on 19 July 1917. The sentence was carried out behind the Town Hall.

That night, as Tim lay in his narrow bed, he dreamed of a soldier in a muddy uniform standing staring at the ground. He woke up to see the moonlight streaming into his room. With a start, he realised that someone was standing over by the wardrobe. The figure took a silent step forward. Tim wasn't surprised to see muddy puttees tightly wound around thin legs. Another step forward and the soldier opened his torn and filthy tunic.

Tim saw a jagged wound across the chest and stomach surrounded by clotted blood. He looked away and back as the figure wavered and faded away. It looked quite solid, but Tim realised that he had not seen its face. Nothing to be done, so Tim rolled over and went back to sleep. He awoke in the morning with the sun streaming through his bedroom window.

Sitting at the breakfast table Tim thought about the wraith he had seen in his bedroom. It appeared to be Private Spettigue, but what was he trying to communicate? Suddenly Tim had it. Spettigue had not died in front of a firing squad at dawn in Poperinge. He had either been bayoneted or ripped apart by a shell.

Offering up a prayer for the man's soul, Tim set off to open the church and say the office. Then he set to digging the vegetable plot in the garden. A couple of rows in his shiny spade unearthed a tarnished disc. Picking it up, he immediately recognised it. Gold in colour with an angel on the back; it was the Victory Medal minus its ribbon. Tim knew where to look; on the edge of the medal were engraved the words: 44587 Pte W Spettigue 8th Bn. DCLI.

So the soldier hadn't been shot by a firing squad at all. He had died fighting near Ypres, and his body had never been found. Tim needed to do some research to put the record straight.

Arriving outside the Keep in Bodmin, Tim parked beside the Railway Station wall. He walked past the DCLI Memorial and passed under the granite gateway before climbing up the granite staircase to the museum.

Sitting in an old armchair in the research room Tim explained the situation to Major Couch, an upright old man with a bristly white moustache.

"Mmm... Let me see. Here are the records of all men shot by firing squad during the Great War. Ah, here we have the DCLI. Yes, a Private W Spettigue 9th Battalion DCLI was due to be shot for cowardice at Poperinge in July 1917. Apparently, he threw down his rifle and ran, striking an officer who tried to stop him. The sentence was commuted to five years in the glasshouse with hard labour."

"Our Private W Spettigue was in the 8th Battalion. I wonder who he really was?"

Back in Goonperran, Tim went to see his old farmer friend George Uren on his farm on the hill above the village. The two men sat on a bench warming their backs against the granite wall of a barn and looking down over a patchwork of small fields enclosed by overgrown granite hedges.

"If I remember right, there were four Spettigue brothers: Jack, James, William, and Walter. Jack was killed first, soon after winning the Military Medal on the Somme. He is on the War Memorial. Two 'Js' and two 'Ws'. This is where it gets confusing.

"Walter came back a few years after the war claiming that his brother had been shot for cowardice. He was an unpleasant man who inherited the house you now live in. He lived there for a few years until he was found dead in the garden. The coroner recorded an open verdict.

"James never showed up in Goonperran. He was heard of in Canada, but then the trail went quiet. I think he couldn't live with the fact that his brother had been executed. Walter couldn't give a toss, but James couldn't face living in the community knowing there was bad blood in the family.

"It's stupid really. Walter had no need to lie about his brother. He didn't learn that William had been killed in action until after the war. He would have inherited the house anyway. So he had to live with the lie he had told until the day he died, an embittered and stubborn man indeed.

"I've never told anyone this story before because this is a close-knit village with many people related. Now the truth is out I think we have a duty to do something about it."

"Yes, indeed, William's name must be put onto the War Memorial below his brother's name. The record must be set straight. I'll see to it."

Gradually, Tim worked the story out in his head as he dug the rich Cornish loam. William's campaign medals must have been sent to Walter's house soon after the Armistice. Walter buried them in the vegetable garden and kept his own medals, proudly polished on the mantelpiece. He would have dug the garden in his old uniform that he had been allowed to keep. Gradually, buttons and badges fell off. When the uniform wore out, he would have burned it in the garden thinking 'Good Riddance'.

At last, Tim looked up and saw the misty form of the soldier again. He had a smile on his face and pointed down to the ground at his feet before vanishing once again. Tim mentally marked the spot and walked over with the spade to find what William had pointed to. A few inches below the surface of the ground was another tarnished disk, this time silver. It was the War Medal, an ounce of solid silver with 44587 Pte W Spettigue 8th Bn DCLI engraved on the rim.

A few weeks later, Tim presented the two shining medals, complete with ribbons, to the Carlyon Arms. They were put in a glass frame and hung on the wall with a brief history, for all to see. In early November of that year, when the name had been carefully carved into the front of the War Memorial, over a hundred people gathered for the Service of Remembrance. Only Tim saw the misty figure standing a little behind the respectful crowd as they bowed their heads in prayer.

Pumphrey's House

Work was progressing well on George Pumphrey's house, left to Tim and then donated to the parish. All the volunteers were back at work with a vengeance, many of them feeling guilty that they could have suspected Tim of groping the choir.

It was the height of summer. The heat lay like a dusty shroud on the village. Usually so open to winds from the south-west Goonperran lay like a limp rag beneath the merciless sun. Dogs and cats lay stretched out in the shade like the mummified remains of the six preserved bodies beneath Bremen Cathedral. Occasionally, they rolled over or scratched themselves to show they still lived.

Tim and Elizabeth, who was down for the weekend from Penzance, wandered along the lane to have a look at the house. Heat radiated in waves from the hot tarmac; even the trees appeared faded and dusty.

The house looked splendid. It even had curtains in the windows. Knocking at the door, Tim called out: "It's us. Let's be having a look, please." The door was opened by Tamsin, daughter of one of the churchwardens.

"It's almost finished. Come and have a look."

The front room looked wonderful with a sofa and chairs from the local Refurnish shop, a rug on the floor and a flat-screen telly against the far wall. A reconditioned log-burning stove was in place in the hearth.

The kitchen looked great too, and the room off the front room. All the plank doors were painted white and a stair carpet, Axminster, no less, led the way to the three small bedrooms and the bathroom, which had a shower in place. Even the antique toilet, reminiscent of Thomas Hardy's at the Old Rectory in St Juliot, was now modern and clean.

"It's wonderful. Liz and I could happily move in here."

"Not unless you were married first," said Denzil, the churchwarden. He was actually half serious for once.

"I must talk to the Parochial Church Council about who should live here. It's absolutely great. Thank you all for your hard work, not only building and labouring but sourcing furniture and fittings."

"Could I suggest the Nancarrow family?" asked Denzil. "Their farm was marginal at best. When their small milking herd was wiped out by TB, they were unable to continue to pay the rent. They have a month of their tenancy left. Young Rob has found a job as a dairyman at the farm at the end of the village, and Jane is studying to be a social worker. The two kids are both at the village primary school and doing well. They would be ideal tenants."

"Good idea, Denzil. We'll see who else needs a house but the Nancarrows are in a bit of a fix. Their farm up on the hill was always tidy and well-run. The soil is poor up there, and the winds come from every quarter. It would be a new start for them."

"One thing though. The garden's still a mess. Should we tidy it up a bit?"

"No, any family who would be prepared to take it on would be good tenants. It's all about stewardship. I know the Nancarrows tried to farm organically, but the landlord had other ideas. Cut the hedges bare, grub out trees, and slap phosphates on the land."

A week later, it was decided. The PCC voted unanimously to put the Nancarrow family in Pumphrey's Cottage, as it would now be called, even though they never came to church. They moved it soon afterwards, bringing all their possessions in a trailer pulled by an ancient tractor that would soon be sold to a collector.

Rob looked at the garden with delight.

"Good deep soil, unlike what we were working up on the hill. Just fine for growing vegetables. Us'll get on with that soon as we'm settled in."

Tim considered the whole project an all-round success story. Not only had the people of the parish pulled together to do the house up, but it now provided a good home for a dependable local family.

All went well for a few hot weeks. At the end of August, the weather showed feeble signs of breaking, but still, no rain came. The Nancarrows' vegetable garden was beginning to shape up, ready for the winter brassicas. Tim looked over the wall as he passed one evening.

"All right, Rob? How's the garden coming along? Found anything yet?"

"Garden's fine, so's the house. The kids love their bedrooms as well as their room downstairs. And yes, I have found something."

He produced a china doll, which was remarkably complete. The painted face looked strangely disturbing with a grimace and slightly crossed eyes.

"Lisa's fallen in love with it, so we'll put it back together and Jane'll sew it some clothes. It'll clean up nicely and live in Lisa's bedroom."

"It looks Victorian. Quite good quality. Strange expression, but maybe it'll look better when it's cleaned up and has grown some hair."

A few days later, Tim was in his study with the window to the garden wide open. He liked to look out at his vegetables and admire the flowers that Elizabeth had planted there. There was a tentative knock at the door. Jane Nancarrow stood on the doorstep, a worried look on her face.

"Come in. Come and sit in the study; it's the coolest room in the house."

She came in and sat down.

"I think our new house is haunted. It could be something we brought with us from the farm, but it only started a few days ago. Things keep falling off shelves and flying across the room. We hear footsteps on the stairs at night, and Lisa's room is very cold."

"I'll come and bless the house if you like. Is Rob alright with that?"

"Yes, he is. We're not really church people, but please could you help us? We love the house and want to stay there forever if we can."

"It doesn't matter if you come to church or not. God is here for everyone. I am His servant and will do everything I can to help you."

That evening, Tim called in at Pumphrey's Cottage. The house felt different: tense and cold. He offered to bless the house and sprinkle holy water in each of the rooms. He realised he should have offered to do this in the first place, soon after the family moved in.

With Rob's agreement, he moved from room to room blessing and sprinkling as he went. The atmosphere lifted until he came to Lisa's room, which was empty since Lisa had moved in with her younger sister Morwenna.

As Tim, followed by all four members of the Nancarrow family, came to the door of Lisa's room, he was unable to enter and pushed back by a blast of icy air. The bed began to sway and danced across the room. A chair fell over, and all Lisa's books were flung onto the floor. Somehow, Tim took a step into the room and blessed it, sprinkling holy water into all four corners. The cold intensified, and the girls ran shrieking down the stairs. Tim came out feeling shaken as the door slammed violently shut behind him.

Back in the front room, he sat shakily down as Jane brought him a cup of tea. Rob comforted the girls in the other room.

"The trouble is confined now to the one bedroom. Lisa is in no way the cause. It isn't a poltergeist, a 'noisy spirit', pulling energy from Lisa. It is something else, brought in recently. What, do you think, could it be?"

"The only thing I can think of is the Victorian doll I dug up in the vegetable garden the other day." Rob's voice drifted in from the other room. "When I was tying the arms and legs back onto the body, the packing needle slipped and gouged the palm of my hand. It went septic, and I had to go to the doctor's. It cost me two days off from work."

Jane added, "And then when I was sewing the clothes onto the doll, I cut myself badly with the same result."

Tim asked Lisa to talk to him.

"Lisa, how do you feel about your new doll? Please be completely honest. Your mum and dad won't be upset, whatever you say."

Lisa was a brave and intelligent girl. "Well... it was alright at first. But the doll's expression seemed to change and became creepy. I had dreams about it every night. It would chase me and was gradually catching up with me. It would shout filthy words and growl at me in my dreams. I don't really like it anymore. It was very kind of Mum and Dad to repair it and dress it, but it seems to be changing and I'm frightened of it now."

"Would you be happy if I took it away, Lisa? Then it couldn't bother you anymore, and life would go back to normal. What do you think?"

"Please take it away. I never want to see it again. Please do that for me."

"I will go and get it right now, and you'll never have to see it or think about it again."

"Thank you, Vicar. I know it will make my room nice again, and the dreams will go away."

"Indeed, they will, Lisa. God will look after you, as He looks after all of us. Rob would you help me with this, please."

The two men went back up the stairs. Tim was praying for strength and guidance as they entered Lisa's cold bedroom. Tim felt strength and energy being drawn from him as he reached out for the doll on the shelf. It felt warm, alive in an evil, sensual way. Tim held it at arm's length as it appeared to squirm in his hand like a warm toad.

Tim wrapped the pulsating doll in a pair of Lisa's socks and carried it downstairs. He took it straight out of the cottage and back to the Rectory, where he placed it on the ground in the garden under a heavy stone. He gathered up dry leaves and twigs and placed the doll on top of the pile. He then lit the small bonfire and watched the smoke rise in the hot air. Then the pile caught with a crackle and the doll shrieked as the flames took it. It writhed before it was consumed. There was a strong smell akin to roast pork before the pile collapsed into ash.

Tim then found a biscuit tin and shovelled all the ash into it. He put the lid on the tin and took it over to the churchyard. Finding a quiet spot on the north side, he buried the tin and its contents with prayers for the family and for himself.

Next day, he was back at Pumphrey's Cottage. The family welcomed him warmly, and Lisa told him about the beautiful dream she had that night. All was well at last. Lisa even had a new doll which had a nice expression that reminded Tim of Elizabeth as well as a soft badger. You couldn't do better than that!

Forches Cross

Elizabeth was down for the weekend staying in the vicarage at Goonperran. Separate bedrooms, of course (Bugger!), Revd. Tim decided it was high time to set a date for their wedding. But, firstly, they had to find a vacancy for a primary school teacher's job in the area. They would never get by on Tim's salary, even living in a tied cottage, St Piran's Vicarage.

Liz loved the village and the church. She even loved the vicarage, a low granite house, which had once been a farmhouse before being given a Delabole slate roof and being sold to the Church of England. She had become very much part of the village. Being Cornish, born and bred, helped, even among the incomers. She was four years younger than Tim and much easier to look at.

At midday, on Saturday, Liz and Tim walked to the Carlyon Arms for a pint. As soon as they entered the bar, they knew that something was wrong. They sat down and ordered a pint and a half of Tinner's.

Arthur Penhale came shyly over to where they sat by the small mullioned window with its view of the green.

"I'm sorry to disturb you, Reverend, Miss, but us'as got a problem a little way out of the village. 'Tis up at Forches Cross. I don't want to tell you about it in 'ere. Could I come over to the vicarage this afternoon?"

"Yes, Arthur, of course. My door is always open. See you later."

"I wonder what that was about," Elizabeth wondered. "It sounds suspiciously like another haunting."

"Oh, no, I hope not. I've got more than enough to do in this parish and the other two without intrusions by the supernatural."

"You seem to be a magnet to ghosts. Perhaps because you know how to deal with them. Well, we'll know soon enough."

That afternoon, Tim and Arthur, a retired farm worker famed for his skill in building Cornish hedges, sat in the study at the vicarage as autumn leaves slowly fell outside the window in the mellow sunlight.

"'Tis like this; folk 'ev seen things up at Forches Cross that nobody should ever see. At night, they hear something swinging in the air, rattling and groaning. When they look, they see the old gibbet that used to stand there years ago. Hanging from it in an iron cage is a collection of bones and rags that used to be a man. But, in the daylight, there is no gibbet nor yet a gallows. Those were taken away years ago when the signposts were put in.

"I've seen 'n meself, times. I saw the head, just a skull with a few wisps of long hair. I think it could be Jake Barnicoat, the thief, hanged over two hundred years ago. But why do us see'n now?"

"I'll go and have a look tonight and see what I can see. Ghosts hold no fear for me. I've seen too many of them to be afraid. They can be a nuisance, though."

"Thank 'ee zur. I wouldn't bother you if it weren't so bleddy orrible. No one should 'ev to see such a thing…"

That evening, after said evensong, Tim and Elizabeth put on their coats against the early autumn chill and walked the half mile up the hill between high hedges to the crossroads.

Elizabeth spoke first, "You know what the word 'Forches' means, don't you?"

"I haven't got a clue. Isn't it just a name?"

"It's never just a name, Tim. 'Forches' means the gallows. They were usually at a crossroads. Often the body of the hanged criminal was tarred and displayed in a sort of cage from a gibbet as an example to everyone. The body would eventually be buried at the crossroads so that its wandering ghost would not know which direction to take."

"How do you know all this, Liz?"

"Been Bodmin Gaol, of course. It's been done up as a really nice hotel, and while not as creepy now, it's even more informative. Too expensive for our honeymoon, though."

"I've managed to escape prison so far so let's not tempt fate!"

Dusk was falling when they reached the crossroads. A light breeze sighed from the west and all was quiet. There were no groans or rattling of chains and no ghastly apparition of a skeletal figure in chains.

"I reckon this one is an urban myth or rather a rural one. We'll come again tomorrow night just before you leave for Truro. It's a nice walk with a great view."

Tim and Liz looked over the darkening fields towards the coast where no less than three lighthouses were visible flashing their intermittent beams across the sea and the fields. They turned to go back down the lane to make supper at the vicarage.

At that point, a faint sigh broke the silence. Both of them heard it but saw nothing.

"Time to go," said Tim. "Before our imaginations play tricks on us. Come on, maid."

The next day was Sunday, a busy day for Tim. The afternoon was clear, so Elizabeth prepared her lessons and Tim finished some paperwork that had been hanging over him like the sword of Damocles, or a gibbet, he found himself thinking. He looked forward to their evening walk.

Faint stars pricked the darkening sky. Arm in arm, Tim and Elizabeth walked up the lane to Forches Cross. Tim was thinking that an evening walk every day would do him good, both physically and mentally.

He felt Liz tense up beside him. She stopped in the middle of the lane.

"Can you see it, Tim?" she asked in a strained voice.

Tim looked up the hill where he saw a faint shape that hadn't been there on the previous night. He could make out a post and a cross-arm at right angles. Dangling from the outstretched arm was an indistinct human shape, which turned slowly in the light breeze.

"Come on, Liz," he said. "Let's get to the bottom of this."

Elizabeth had never lacked courage, and Tim wasn't afraid of what lay at the top of the hill. They walked up to the crossroads. By then, the moon was up but the figure, and the gibbet cast no shadow.

They could make out rusty hoops holding the body together, and ribs reflected the moonlight. The right arm had fallen to the bottom of the cage. A withered hand hung out as if in supplication. The skull could be clearly seen, and the few remaining teeth were discoloured. Hanks of hair hung over the forehead, but both eyes had gone. Empty eye sockets were pools of darkness.

"Well, we've seen it. What now?" asked Elizabeth.

"It's just an image. There's no intelligence or malice present. It's a place ghost, an image from the past that certain people can see and others can't. I'm surprised that we both can see it. But that's as far as it goes."

"What do we do now?"

"I think I know but I must talk to Frank first. This won't be a Deliverance or exorcism job, but something must be done. Our criminal friend isn't a pleasant sight. He could scare the horses."

"I'm not scared, but the image certainly isn't pleasant. I won't forget it in a hurry."

Next day, Tim was on the phone with Frank, explaining the situation and asking for his advice. Frank came over that evening from his parish in Bodmin.

"I think we have a classic haunting here. An image with no interaction with the people seeing it. No communication, but there is a message. Have you got a spade? I think we're about to do something illegal."

Producing his trusty Cornish spade, Tim knew what they had to do. He knew it had to be done in daylight and quickly. After a quick pasty and cup of tea in the vicarage kitchen, the two priests set out with a spade and Frank's battered leather Gladstone bag. First, Tim fed his black cat, Crowley.

Walking up the hill, Tim and Frank decided which prayers they would use. But, first, there was digging to be done. Frank kept watch while Tim dug exploratory pits in the verges at the crossroads. He soon struck lucky. Close to the magnificent cast iron sign that had four arms pointing down four lanes he unearthed the knob of a long bone.

"Looks human," remarked Frank. "And, more important, it looks old. We don't want to fall foul of the law. Two clergymen digging up human remains and not reporting them could land us in court."

"Would a suspended sentence be appropriate here," replied Tim. "Like our hanged friend Jack Barnicoat. Let's see how much of him we can find without causing a scandal."

In a few minutes, the two men had enough long bones, splintered ribs and even part of a skull to establish that they had found their man. This was finally confirmed by the paper-thin rusted manacles that encircled one of the ankle bones.

Tim produced an old army kitbag kept back from the QM's stores when he left the army. Perhaps it was, in small measure, Tim's revenge for what the army had put him through in hot, dusty countries where nearly everyone had been trying to kill him. The bones were carefully placed in the kitbag when no more could be found.

Tim then carefully put back the earth and replaced the turf, patting it down with the space so that it looked undisturbed. Then prayers were said for the dead and for the repose of the soul of Jake Barnicoat, hanged, apparently, for stealing half a loaf of bread in the village.

The two men trudged down the hill with the knowledge that the oppressive feeling at the crossroads had lifted. Two hundred yards down the lane, they saw a police car approaching and stood to the side of the road.

"You two look most suspicious," said Sergeant Burnett. "Been cleaning out a buddle hole, I'll bet."

"Something like that," Tim said evasively.

"If I didn't know that you two were vicars I'd ask you a few more questions," joked the policeman. "Take care."

There was one more job to be done. As the rising wind blew through bent thorn trees, Tim dig a square hole in a corner of the churchyard, reverently placing in the bones and saying the committal part of the funeral service. He had put on his stole, as had Frank. Nobody witnessed the burial. Had they done so they would have hurried quietly away.

Tim explained the whole situation to Elizabeth on the phone that night.

"All's well that ends well," she said. "Now what about us? We've solved other people's problems, and now, it's time we decided when our wedding will take place."

Tim's answer delighted the girl on the other end of the telephone.

Away with the Fairies

Elizabeth was in Goonperran for a couple of days for the interview. She had applied for the post of deputy head at St Piran's Church of England primary school and had been shortlisted. Tim had stepped back from the process, as was only proper. Elizabeth was staying two nights at the Carlyon Arms, much to the amusement of the parish. The interview was the next day, and she didn't have a clue what her chances were.

After supper, she sat in the vicarage in front of the newly installed woodburner feeling warm for once. She glanced idly at that day's copy of the Western Morning News.

"Tim, there's something here about Goonperran."

"Really, my love? Please read it out."

"Extraordinary Photographs at Goonperran. Fairies Dancing in the Dusk.

"By our Cornwall Correspondent Tristan Trewhella: Two teenage girls in Goonperran claim to have photographed fairies dancing on the stretch of moorland just north of the village. Tamsin and Morwenna Bennets said they saw the wee folk on five consecutive nights last week. On the fifth evening, they took their phones and photographed them. The results show a ring of tiny winged creatures appearing to dance in a circle in the dusk. There are seven photos, all of which show different fairies and a number of slightly larger gnomes sitting behind them.

"The girls and their parents agreed to have the photos examined in a laboratory to prove their veracity. Today, the lab at the University of Penwith at Tremough contacted us with their results: "We can find no signs of trickery in any of these photographs. They have not been Photoshopped or interfered with in any way. We examined all the laptops and tablets belonging to the Bennets family and found no trace of any doctoring of the photos. We can only conclude that these images are genuine. The other possibility is that the family could have used an advanced form of technology unknown to us but this is unlikely as we are at the cutting edge of image technology."

"Yes," said Tim. "There's always a get-out clause in these reports."

"That's very cynical from a man of faith."

"Perhaps, but fairies have no place in our holy religion."

Elizabeth laughed.

"I just hope we don't get overrun with emmets and people looking for elves, gnomes and fairies. Let's have a look at the photos."

Elizabeth passed them over to him. When he saw them, he gasped.

"Darn clever, these maids. I don't know how they did it, but the results are very convincing. Have a look."

"I already did and really don't know what to make of them…"

The three colour photos in the paper showed what appeared to be three-dimensional figures dressed in gauzy dresses that were rather dirty. They had transparent wings and danced in a circle. The figures at the front were just off the short turf while the ones at the back were a couple of feet above the ground, their wings whirring. Each had a different expression of joy on their faces. The gnomes who sat behind on the turf appeared to be enjoying the show which was backlit by the sinking red orb of the autumn sun.

The figures appeared to be solid and animated, not flat or two-dimensional.

"Extraordinary!" Elizabeth remarked.

"I hope they don't ask you what you think of them at the interview tomorrow."

"If they do I'll say, they're interesting but that the jury's out. I must go now. I need my beauty sleep if I'm to make any sense tomorrow in this pixilated parish."

Before going to sleep, Tim prayed for the interview on the morrow and for the girls who took the photos. God's will be done!

Next day, Tim said the offices in church and did his rounds of visiting while trying not to think of Elizabeth sitting facing five governors of the school, the Head Teacher, and a representative of Cornwall County Council Education Committee. He thought privately that Cornwall is not a county but a Duchy.

As he was working in his office at tea time, the phone rang. It was Elizabeth:

"They gave me the job! I'm delighted by the school and everything to do with it. It will be a challenge and a big step up. I've accepted it after keeping them waiting for all of ten minutes!"

"Well done, Liz. Proper job. I thought they'd give it to you. You'll do it really well. This evening, we must go to the Carlyon Arms to celebrate and talk about a date for the wedding."

The phone rang again. It was Rob Bennets:

"Vicar, we need to talk to you about these photos. We've got visitors in the lane outside and the Press and TV cameras everywhere. I talked very seriously to the girls, and they assured me that these photos are not a hoax. I gave them every chance to own up before it got too big for us, but they stand firm, and I believe them."

"I'll come over at ten tomorrow, and we can talk about it. I'll need to talk to the girls as well. Don't worry, I won't give them a hard time. But I have a few questions to ask them. We can take it from there and decide what can be done about it. See you tomorrow, Rob."

Next morning, Tim walked briskly over to the Bennets' farm below the moor. He sat down in the kitchen in front of the Cornish range, which glowed in the crisp autumn morning.

"I know how these photos got into the paper. One of my girls shared the images with a friend who then sent them straight to the WMN. Our girls would never have done that. Neither would they have told lies. They were brought up to be straight and honest. I believe what they say. But what on earth did they photograph?

"There are stories of fairies and knockers and cobbolds in the old tin mines, but no one has believed in them for years. They're great stories for a dark winter's night or in the pub but I've never seen piskies or such creatures."

"I can't make it out either. Please may I talk to the girls? I'd like you to stay with us when I do if that's alright."

Tamsin and Morwenna were fetched from their rooms. Because of all the fuss, they had been kept home from school. Tamsin was sixteen and studying for four A Levels at the local comprehensive school, Morwenna was fourteen and, like her older sister, exuded common sense and intelligence.

"Please may I see the prints of the seven photos?" Tim asked.

The girls fetched the images and set them out in order on the kitchen table. Tim looked carefully at each one. He saw solid but ethereal tiny figures dancing in a circle. Each photo led on to the next. But, in the last image, a dark figure lurked in the background.

"What is the figure behind the gnomes?" Tim asked.

"We haven't seen it before. It wasn't there last time we looked. I don't like the look of it at all!"

The sinister figure seemed to be gaining definition. It loomed in the background. Its head was bald and wrinkled with dark brows and a sinister leering light emanating from its piercing eyes. It made Tim think of Aleister Crowley.

"We must burn these photos immediately. A demon, or evil spirit is trying to gain access to us. The bait was the images of dancing fairies. There are no fairies apart from in the mind of the demon."

"What are we to do? This is very frightening. I wish we had never taken those photographs."

"We must all pray together. God will deliver us from persecution. It is not too late. Remember Peter Pan. If you don't believe in fairies, then they die. As they didn't exist in the first place they can't die. They are a figment of the imagination but in this case a figment of Satan's imagination. Kill them off and you wound Satan. Pretend it was all a joke."

The family prayed together, silently and with words from Tim. A great weight was lifted from the family. But what to do about the photos in the papers? Tim spoke at last:

"What we do is nothing. Pretend it never happened. Don't answer any questions and let people think what they want. It will soon go away, a nine days' wonder. Take a holiday if you can. When you come back, it will all be forgotten. Never mention it again. Even if they offer you money, say nothing. The WMN won't do that, they're ethical. But others will get out their chequebooks. Take nothing and say nothing. The matter is closed."

That evening Tim and Elizabeth walked up the long hill that led to the moor. It was a glorious evening. The crowds around the farm had dispersed. The film cameras and radio vans had gone. Cornish people can keep a secret.

Elizabeth was still glowing from the result of her interview. Then a frown creased her forehead.

"Tim, I've just remembered something. The Cottingly Fairies. Two young girls took some photos with their father's camera in a dell by a stream behind their house in Yorkshire. They showed them to friends and the news got out. An important doctor believed they had taken authentic pictures of actual fairies. He went on a lecture tour and managed to convince no less a person than Sir Arthur Conan Doyle who believed in the fairies in the photos until the day he died.

"Here, on my phone. I've brought up the photos. Convincing, aren't they?

"Just before they died one of the girls, now an old lady, admitted that the photos had been faked. They had done it for a joke by cutting out illustrations from a children's book of fairy stories and from Pear's Soap wrappers. Once people began to believe them they couldn't admit the truth. So they went through their lives living a lie."

"The Devil had a hand in that little episode as well it seems. Now he's tried again. He's a plagiarist as well as a liar and a deceiver. Let's see if we can see any fairies up here."

Of course, there was nothing to be seen. But the odd blade of grass twitched by itself and the odd leaf moved as if blown by a breeze. Tim turned to Elizabeth.

"By the way, how about 10 March? Truro Cathedral. Be there?"

"Of course! I thought you'd never get around to it! How did you manage the cathedral?"

"The Dean was a senior officer in my regiment. He owed me a few favours from Iraq. If I hadn't pushed him over in the road when he was about to tread on a mine, he and I wouldn't be here to tell the tale. He wasn't happy at the time and called me names no cleric would use today. Like the fairies, it's water under the bridge."

Black and White

Winter had arrived in Goonperran. January dragged itself towards February with cold east winds and frosty mornings. Some days the frost lingered permanently in the hedge bottoms and in the places untouched by the warmth of the sun.

It was on a cold Monday morning that Revd. Tim wrapped himself in his warm burial cloak and walked through frosty lanes to say the morning office at St Piran's church. Inside the church, it was even colder than outside. *Dead air*, thought Tim. His breath made a cloud as he said matins.

Pulling the heavy church door closed behind him, Tim cast his eye around the frosty churchyard. A dead robin lay on the grass and Tim noticed little twig crosses on a number of the graves. He counted thirteen, gathering them up after noting on whose graves they had been placed. Five of the marked graves belonged to the Pelleymounter family, the other seven seemed more randomly placed.

Each cross was two hawthorn twigs tied together with red wool. Tim suspected some sort of pagan rite or even witchcraft. He determined that he would burn most of the crosses but keep two for further reference.

Back in the Vicarage Tim opened the wood-burning stove that had been a wedding present from the parish and threw eleven of the crosses in, watching them catch and burned almost instantaneously. *What a wonderful present the stove had been*, he thought.

He realised now what he needed to do. Pulling out his battered phone he rang Dr Pellymounter and asked if he could visit her. The answer being an enthusiastic affirmative he wrapped himself once more in the cloak and set out for the other end of the village, aware of the rooks gathering in the bare trees around the church.

He had not visited Dr, actually Professor, Pelleymounter before. She had always made it quite clear that she had little time for the hurch, even though she was happy to talk to the vicar. Apparently, she was a formidable lady, never married, who had retired to the village from which her family had originally come.

She lived alone at the far end of the village in a surprisingly large Georgian house. Tim noticed a weather vane above the stables that showed a witch riding a broomstick, an unusual object for Goonperran.

The front door opened and a large, humorous-looking lady in late middle age ushered Tim into the warm kitchen where some very nice coffee was percolating. A large Aga provided warmth and two black cats were stretched out in front of it.

"Good morning Professor," Tim said formerly.

"Professor bollocks!" Dr Pelleymounter replied. "Call me Florence. Life's too short for formality. I left that title behind when I retired."

"May I ask what you were the professor of?" asked Tim. "I've always been curious."

"I had the great pleasure to be a professor of witchcraft studies at the University of Exeter. Hence the weather vane, a present from the faculty when I retired. I expect they think that I now practise what I preached."

"And do you, might I ask?"

"Good Lord, no! But I know that there is a lot of it about, particularly in this part of the world."

"That's exactly what I have come to see you about. I found thirteen crosses on thirteen different graves in the churchyard this morning. Five of them were on the graves of members of your family. I've come to see what can be done about them."

"In my experience, they are a form of curse, or at least a warning. I cannot think what I might have done to upset the local witch for the life of me."

"Who is the local witch in Goonperran?"

"From what I hear it's Sal Scratch. Her name is actually Sally Screech. She lives in one of the old council houses at the other end of the village. From what I hear she isn't just a white witch either. She never cleans or tidies her house and has the reputation of being a 'good hater'. I wonder what I've done to upset her."

"I could go and have a word with her if you like. We can't have graves desecrated and interfered with."

"She's not a woman to be crossed. She's very direct. People are afraid of her so tread carefully. She has even less time for the church than I do. But don't let that bother you. You're always welcome here and if I can help you I will. I don't bite, you know."

A few minutes later Tim let himself out. He had enjoyed his talk with Florence Pelleymounter and had rather taken to the lady. He set off to the other end of the village to talk to Sal Scratch. A watery sun cast weak shadows and no appreciable warmth as Tim walked briskly through the village.

The other end of the village was generally neat, but Sally Screech's house stood out as neglected and dismal. There was no weather vane there. A weedy and neglected front garden led up to the peeling paint of the front door. Filthy and torn curtains hung in the smeared windows. Tim knocked on the door. He heard shuffling footsteps approach and unlock the door. Unusual to lock a front door during the day in Goonperran.

The woman who opened the door was short and grimy. Grey hair straggled from her head. Her face was wrinkled and her expression suspicious and hostile.

"Oh, the vicar. Well, you'd better come in," she said grudgingly, holding the door open a crack. A stale smell reached Tim's nostrils, but he followed the woman into the untidy front room.

"Sit 'ee down, will 'ee," she said. Then she sat down in an ancient sagging armchair.

"What do'ee want?"

"I'm here about the crosses in the churchyard. Do you know anything about them?"

"I most certainly do. I put 'em there. That Pelleymounter woman is prying into what I do. 'Er has no business doing that. So I put a warning on her family's graves. I can't abide 'er."

Tim let the woman ramble on while casting his eyes around the room. He saw a faded photograph of Aleister Crowley in a frame on the wall with Crowley's phallic signature below it. Also, on the wall was an embroidered sampler with the faint words 'Do what thou will be the whole of the law'.

"Do you know who that photo is of?" Tim asked.

"Yes, the Great Beast 666, the Master."

"Are you a Satanist? I must ask this in order to understand."

"Of course, I am, you daft bugger! And a black witch. I put curses on people, and they die. 'Tis what I do and have always done. Why am I entertaining a priest in my house? I have nothing to say to you! Get out of my house you 'orrible bastard! I'll 'ave no truck with you! Satan is king. He will prevail! Get out you ugly sod!"

"Good day, Mrs Screech. I've been called much worse in the army. May God bless you."

"Arseholes! Don't show your face here again. You won't be welcome. Now sod off!"

"Off I sod. Goodbye, Mrs Screech."

Tim was shocked and amused at the same time. But he now knew where the roots of the problem lay. He might need to consult Frank on this matter.

Next day, he visited Dr Pelleymounter again. He was horrified to see that she had lost weight and was looking thoroughly pulled over.

"Come in, I think I might need your help. Please sit and listen to me and tell me what you think."

"Of course Florence. It's what I'm here for."

Once more they sat in the warm kitchen drinking tea. Dr Pelleymounter fixed Tim with bloodshot eyes.

"Tim, I feel like someone who is having her life force diminished. I feel tired, irritable, and thoroughly crappy. It could be the curse put on me by Sal Scratch. I think I need your help with this…"

"Of course, Florence. Are you happy to pray with me?"

"I'll try anything to lift this curse. Even Christianity!"

Tim said some prayers for the deliverance of Florence from the evil eye. He spent some time explaining what he was doing. An aura of peace descended on the house.

"There is one thing more I must do today to lift this curse. I must go back and visit Sal Scratch and tell her what I have done. It won't be pleasant, but I must complete what I have begun."

"Thank you, Tim, for listening and for trying to do what you can to help me. Come back and tell me what you find. The theory and practice of black magic are strange and frightening. I never thought that I would experience anything like this."

Tim walked back through the chilly village to Sal Scratch's house which stood out on the estate like a wart on a witch's nose. He knocked at the open door but wasn't invited in. He knocked again but could only hear a faint creaking sound. Pushing open the door, he went in. He entered the dark hall and looked up at the stairwell.

What he saw there he would never forget. Swinging lazily in the cold draft from the door was an indistinct figure hanging from a rope. Sal Scratch had hanged herself in the stairwell. Intent on saving life Tim ran up the stairs. He felt for a pulse on the dangling wrist, but the body was stone cold. He was tempted to cut her down but pulled out his phone and called the police. Then he sat on the front doorstep and waited, glad he hadn't looked at the face.

The following Sunday Tim was surprised to see Dr Pelleymounter at the morning service. He had phoned her to tell her what had happened. She looked well and alert. After the service, she took him aside.

"Tim, I was wrong about the church. I've studied religions of various sorts all my life, but this is the first time I've felt connected. Please consider me a part of the congregation from now on. May God's name be praised."

A few weeks later there was a knock on the vicarage door. It Was Florence, for once looking shy.

"Come in. You're always welcome, as you would be if you never darkened the doors of St Piran's. What can I do for you?"

Florence, now sitting in the kitchen in front of the wood burner, looked intently at Tim.

"I'd like you to sponsor me as a lay reader. But first I need to be baptised and confirmed. Could you see to that, please?"

"Of course, Florence, I'd be delighted to. There will be interviews with the Diocesan Selection Board. It shouldn't be a problem for you. I think you'll be fine!"

When it came to funerals Tim insisted on having Sal Scratch's in St Piran's. He also insisted on her being buried in the cemetery. He prayed for her immortal soul every day.

Spectres at the Wedding

It had been a wet and windy winter in North Cornwall, with storm bands coming in from the Atlantic to batter the village and in particular, the church. Christmas had come and gone, now just a memory of candles, carols, and Christingles. The green fuse of spring had been lit with snowdrops and early daffodils coming into flower in the hedges and gardens of Goonperran.

Revd. Tim and Elizabeth were preparing for their wedding in Truro Cathedral. Elizabeth was happy working as deputy head at the village primary school. It was well-run by enthusiastic people and the children were making good progress. She had taken a room with the Wadge family and was comfortable and well looked after.

The first of March was St David's Day, always a turning point towards spring. Of even more significance was 5 March, St Piran's Day, the village's patronal festival. The black and white flag was run up on the church tower and the church was decorated with flowers. A special service was held with a sit-down lunch in church. Many people who normally didn't come to church were there. Tim preached a lively sermon on the life of St Piran, pointing out that the millstone on which he sailed over from Ireland was probably a coracle and that he had founded what is probably the oldest church building in Britain. His example as a missionary among the heathen was a good one, and his memory was kept alive all over the Granite Kingdom, especially on 5 March.

Most nights Tim dreamed of his past life, a sort of pre-nuptial review of his tender conscience. He felt that his impending marriage would help him turn his back on his past transgressions. He had told everything of his past life, good and bad, to Elizabeth, not wanting her to find anything out from anyone else. He was gratified to be accepted for what he was, a reformed sinner who was trying his best to stay on the straight and narrow, by the grace of God.

The morning of 10 March finally arrived. It was Wedding Day at last. Tim and Elizabeth arrived separately in Truro, dressed to the nines. Both felt nervous: Tim in his best clerical suit and Elizabeth in a beautiful white wedding dress. She wondered if Tim snored, whether he got up frequently in the night for a pee, whether he talked in his sleep. She waited in the hotel where the reception would be held with her bridesmaids, all of whom were sisters and cousins from all over Cornwall. Her parents were there as well as her aunts and uncles.

Tim was sitting in a vestry in the cathedral, waiting with the Dean as the nave filled with parishioners and relatives. His parents were sitting in the front row, stiff in their smart new clothes.

"Right, Tim," said the Dean. "On parade. Always five minutes before the start time. Let's move it."

Tim's heart gave a great leap. He looked forward to the ceremony being over so that he could be quietly alone with Liz.

So Tim found himself sitting in a chair at the crossing, waiting for his bride to be brought to him by her father. Frank, his best man sat in a chair a few yards away. Tim looked at the sea of faces in front of him before raising his eyes to the open west door where soon the woman with whom he would spend the rest of his life would enter the cathedral.

He tried not to look too closely at the people in front of him. Above him, stone vaults soared up into the lofty roof space. Light and air were all about him. He glanced over at the north aisle where the new monument to the great Cornish poet Charles Causley had been recently installed. Then his eye was drawn to a distant movement at the west door.

A woman's figure entered quietly. She was alone and appeared shadowy. She walked silently up the aisle followed by others, all silent and in single file. Tim realised, with a start that he managed to conceal, that she was one of his past lovers. Now approaching the crossing she bowed slightly and smiled at Tim before turning into the north aisle and gradually becoming transparent before vanishing. The other women followed; all dressed differently; some were blond; some dark; all were attractive.

Each of the women gave a slight bow and turned either right or left before becoming opaque and vanishing. Each gave Tim a smile of encouragement. The last few women had blank faces with no features but still gave the impression of encouragement. Tim remained calm. This he took as a sign of approval.

He glanced down at the front row of the nave, the place where his parents and relations should be. What he saw was somewhat different; he saw soldiers in filthy and torn combats sitting in a row. He recognised all of them, the living and the dead. There was Sergeant Atkins with one leg and one arm off and Corporal Hatch with blood streaming down his face. Each gave him a grin and a thumbs up. The soldiers who still lived were in their best Number Two uniforms rather than dusty and bloody torn camo. They also smiled up at him and gave the thumbs up.

Tim would never share this vision with anyone. He blinked and the soldiers vanished, to be replaced by his father sitting with his large rough hands on his knees and his mother staring at the west window with its incongruous round blue patch. His uncles and aunts, farming and fishing people and ex-tin miners were all sitting expectantly. Frank continued to sit quietly in his chair completely unaware of what Tim had seen.

Then the heavy bell stuck three high in the spire and Elizabeth was there at the west door on her father's arm. They briefly blocked out the sunlight before the organ started playing Pachelbel. Then they walked slowly forward up the centre of the nave to meet Tim at the crossing.

The service went well. No rings were dropped, nobody fainted, and the vows were spoken out good and loud, as they should be. The reception at the Three Rivers Hotel was simple and enjoyable. Tim was pleased to see that his parents and Elizabeth's parents got on very well. Tim's father and mother had done well. With little education, but lots of hard work, they had stayed on the council estate in Penzance where they had settled, bought their house, and seen the area come up from being a rough no-go area to a pleasant area in which to live. They had been a good example, tending a large vegetable garden behind the house, keeping everything tidy, and helping the neighbours with all sorts of problems. Tim was proud of his parents and they, a little bemused by his priestly calling, were proud of him.

Elizabeth's parents were more middle class but just as down to earth. They owned their house in Truro and both worked at County Hall. Her two younger sisters were there as bridesmaids. Tim was an only child and welcomed being part of a large extended family.

On the last day of their short honeymoon, Tim and Liz woke up in an enormous bed in the Headland Hotel in Newquay. As Tim luxuriantly wiggled his toes he caught Elizabeth looking at the wedding ring on her left hand.

"My Gran told me that Cornish women always wore their wedding rings on their thumbs," he said.

"Silly! Did she wear a wedding ring? Was she actually married?"

"Touche," Tim replied. "I don't think I ever looked. She came from Bodmin, you know. She was a Wadge, like the folk in the village. Another thing she used to say is that if you went to Bodmin it was to join the army, if you were sent to

Bodmin it was to go to the lunatic asylum, and if you were taken to Bodmin it was to the prison."

"I've heard that surname before. Wasn't there a Selina Wadge who was hanged at Bodmin Gaol for infanticide?"

"Yes, there was. She must have been a relation, coming from Altarnun as she did."

"I think she was the last woman hanged there in public. What a distinguished family!"

At breakfast, Tim and Elizabeth talked about the wedding and what it meant to them. She had not been really nervous and had been determined to be at the cathedral on time. Then she asked Tim a leading question:

"Tim, when you were waiting for me to come in at the west door did your past life flash before your eyes as it is supposed to do when you are drowning? Mine did and I welcomed it, knowing that any past mistakes were now firmly in the past."

"Yes, you could say that! A whole page was firmly turned as I waited for you. We can now look forward to a new life in familiar surroundings."

Lighten Our Darkness

It was a Friday evening in late spring, the end of the working week for Elizabeth but not for Revd. Tim. To celebrate the couple went out to the Carlyon Arms for a pint of Tinners'. They had both earned it and the visit gave Tim the opportunity to talk to members of his parish who didn't often turn up at church on a Sunday.

They were given a good welcome in the snug bar. After ordering, they sat down by the fire and listened to the man who was holding forth.

"'T'was like this," he said. "I was on my way home from a job at Farmer Uren's place the other evening when I saw these 'ere lights dancing all over the moor and shining bright in the dusk. I couldn't make out what they were so I stopped and stood looking over the hedge at them. They wuz bouncing around and stopping before starting up again and whirling all over the place. What do you think they be, Reverend?"

"They could be marsh gas burning and going out, reigniting and acting like a will o' wisp."

"I 'ev 'eard that they be showing the whereabouts of hidden treasure," said Ernie Wise from beneath his greasy cloth cap.

"And I 'ev 'eard they could be piskies," added Rose the postman's wife.

Tim said: "We'll have a walk after supper and see what this is all about. I love a mystery, especially one that doesn't involve ghosts, for a change."

The talk ebbed and flowed under the low ceiling of the pub. Tim and Elizabeth loved hearing the voices they had always heard saying curious things that excited their imaginations. Then they left the pub for their tea in the vicarage.

When Tim had washed up he fed the voracious black cat Crowley and pulled on his old camo jacket. Elizabeth put on her coat, and they walked out into the dusk. After crossing the village, they headed uphill towards the edge of the moor. It was a bracing walk with the sun sinking to their right in the west.

Reaching the edge of the rough ground they turned round to look at the silver expanse of the sea to the north. A small coaster lay at anchor not far off the coast, its riding lights just visible.

"That's strange," said Tim. "Ships don't usually anchor off the coast just there. It's dangerous. The wind and the currents come in fast, and there are no harbours for quite a stretch."

"I wonder if it's in trouble. Let's phone the coastguard when we get back."

They turned round to look at the darkening moorland.

"Look!" Elizabeth exclaimed. "I can see some of those lights they were talking about in the pub. They really are quite strange!"

"By gar! So can I! Let's stand here a while and see what they do."

The lights seemed to bob up and down changing in intensity as they did so. From time to time one would rise up and swoop over the gorse and heather before sinking down again. They were mainly blue and orange, and some were light green. They seldom kept still but performed a crazy dance that seemed to have no rhyme or reason.

Tim held Elizabeth's hand. She was the delight of his life, and he loved being married to her. She felt the same about him. Every shared experience brought them closer together. They felt no fear, only wonder at these charming lights that danced all over the tops of the moorland hills.

"Orbs," said Tim. "Some sort of energy, undoubtedly natural. There's no meaning in them, no intelligence."

"Marsh gas? But it's been so dry this spring. What fun!"

After twenty minutes, the lights began to lose intensity and started to wink out as they dropped into the heather.

"Time to go," said Tim. "Tea will be ready."

The next day, Saturday, Tim answered the phone in his study.

"Frank! 'Ow be? I haven't heard from you for too long. Everything is fine here. A few orbs on the moor but no diabolic manifestations, thank God."

"That's really what I'm ringing you about. I've just heard from the Archdeacon that the cathedral wants to make me a

Canon Chancellor. This means that I'll spend half my time at the cathedral and half in my parish. We're looking for a new Deliverance Minister and you spring to mind. No more money, I'm afraid, but your experience in the matter makes you the ideal person for it. What do you think?"

"Bleddy hell! I'll have to think about it and talk to Liz. I must admit that I am tempted; it's an interesting role to have. I'm not at all ambitious. I don't want to be rural dean or even archdeacon. I have more than enough to do in these three parishes. But someone has to do the job and, at least I have had some experience. By the way, congratulations! A well-deserved promotion!"

"Do let me know what you decide."

The coastguard thanked Tim for his enquiry and told him that the ship at anchor off the coast was the MV Island Trader, registered in the Bahamas, Captain Mould, master. It was there for engine repairs that should take no more than a day or two. Coastguards were keeping an eye on it, particularly since she hadn't reported that she had anchored there.

On Saturday evening, Tim and Elizabeth enjoyed another evening stroll up the lane to the moor's edge. They like the contrast between the small stone-hedged fields and the granite spine of Cornwall asserting itself like bones through flesh.

The orbs were there again. This time they were acting differently. Instead of darting about all over the moor they were slowly rising and falling in one place. As each one rose it became brighter, dimming down as it fell back in the dimpsy.

Elizabeth spoke first:

"It's as if they had some kind of intelligence and were trying to show us something. We must mark the spot where they rise and fall."

"That's easy. It's hollow where the old tin mine working. All the buildings have gone, the stone stolen for various building projects a long time ago. Wheal Lizzy, 'twas known as and always had the reputation of being an unlucky mine. 'Tis reputed to be haunted, by the way…"

"Time to head back, before the ghosties and long-legged beasties get hold of us."

"Or our imaginations," added Tim, putting a protective arm around his wife.

On turning, they couldn't help but see a light flashing from the ship to someone on shore. It couldn't have been Morse Code, that was long out of date. So it must have been some sort of signal to someone on the cliff. Most irregular when radio could have been used.

"I smell a rat," said Tim. "Come on, we must report this."

Back in the Vicarage Tim put in a call to Police Headquarters at Bodmin.

"Hello, could I speak to DCI Bunting, please? It's a matter of some urgency."

Soon a voice was heard from the other end of the line:

"Hello, Tim. What can I do for you?"

Bunting was an old army buddy of Tim's, his commanding officer in Iraq.

"There's a ship, the MV Island Trader, anchored just off Penjowler Head. She didn't want anyone to know she was there. I saw she was signalling by lamp to someone on the cliff. I'm pretty sure that a smuggling operation is going on.

"If you send some men quietly up to Wheal Lizzy, just up on the moor above Goonperran, there's a fair chance that you'll catch someone. There's been some activity up there the last couple of nights."

"If anyone else had told me this I'd doubt their sanity, but as it's you I'll follow your hunch and act on it. Keep everyone away from the area. I'll send some armed police officers up there. Thank you for the tip-off. If nothing comes of it, you'll owe us several pints of Tinners'."

"Fair enough. I'll be up there watching so prepare your men not to shoot or arrest me. I'll make sure nobody else is up there."

The Sunday evening Tim walked up to the moor alone, leaving Elizabeth with lesson plans and objectives for the coming week to prepare. She cautioned him to be careful, remembering his army training and experience.

Wearing an old set of combats and thinking that 'thou shall not steal', even from the British Army, was one of the Ten Commandments, Tim hid in the bracket. He made sure his mobile phone was switched off and lay listening and watchful. He had no idea if the police were there or not.

Ten minutes later his patience was rewarded. A police Landrover drove up a track onto the moor. But the three men who got out were not policemen. They were armed, but their lack of training showed immediately. He could hear every word they said. Their accents were Caribbean, and they made their way to the old mineshaft, unlocking the rusty steel door which swung back noisily on its corroded hinges.

"Don't make so much bloody noise, Marlon!"

"There's nobody up here, man, only duppies and pixies."

Packets were transferred from the Landrover to the mine, and Marlon was in the act of locking the steel door when a hoarse voice shouted: "Police! Stay exactly where you are. Do not move! We are armed and will shoot if you attempt to resist. Throw down your arms and lie down immediately!"

Five heavily armed police officers, unrecognisable in their protective gear, rose out of the heather, their weapons trained on the three skinny men. The smugglers gave up without a struggle and were handcuffed and taken away.

A hoarse voice called out: "Tim, show yourself! We've got three suspects in custody. All clear now."

Tim rose like a wraith out of the heather, only a few yards from the action.

"A bunch of amateurs. You have to feel sorry for them in a way. It could be a case of modern slavery."

"Turn round and look out to sea."

Tim did so and saw two police RIBs heading for the ship, searchlights trained on the decks and the bridge. It was all over in a matter of minutes. Tim could only imagine what was happening out to sea, but he had every confidence that the police had got their man.

Behind, on the moor, the packets were being carefully photographed and examined before being put in the back of a genuine police Landrover, watched over by two anonymous armed policemen.

"Heroin and Cocaine, millions of pounds worth! Well done Tim! I think the Tinners' will be on us." DCI Bunting pulled down his balaclava and grinned from ear to ear.

Next day, after Tim had explained everything to Elizabeth, he phoned Dr Pelleymounter.

"Florence, may I come in a minute and have a word with you? You might be able to help me sort something out in my mind."

"Of course. Great to see you, Tim. Coffee's on."

Sitting once again in Florence's tidy kitchen Tim asked:

"Orbs! What can you tell me about them?"

"There are two kinds: the kind that appears in photographs, which can be usually explained by light entering the camera and the other kind that shows some sort of intelligence that is trying to communicate some knowledge previously unknown to the watcher."

Tim explained what had happened on the last three evenings on the edge of the moor.

"Well," concluded Florence. "You thought that fairies didn't exist anymore. They may not show themselves flying around or dancing in the glens. But they might manifest themselves as glowing orbs."

"Lights to lighten the Gentiles," said Tim.

"Precisely!"

A Blast from the Past

Early summer in Goonperran was delightful. Soft breezes caressed the new leaves which glowed with a fresh green that had not yet become dusty. The few second homeowners in the parish came to open up their neglected houses and park their expensive Chelsea Tractors in the narrow lanes.

Elizabeth was happily anticipating a break from work at half term. The summer term was always a long one with lots of fun activities as well as assessments and preparing the senior class for secondary school. She loved her job and put a lot into it. The introduction of classes in the Cornish language was popular but required a lot of preparation to keep on top of the difficult language. A break would be very welcome.

Revd. Tim was owed some time off, so the couple had planned to spend a few days in England. They were going to Wales for a complete break for a few days. So it came as a complete surprise when a woman arrived on the weekly bus from St Austell asking the way to the vicarage.

Tim and Elizabeth were about to put their suitcases into Elizabeth's battered Renault when there was a knock on the door. Tim opened it to a rather rough-looking young woman who stood holding the hand of a small child with a runny nose. She seemed familiar to Tim. He realised with a start that he knew her and instantly wished he didn't.

"Remember me?" the woman said. "Tamsin Murphy. We were lovers once. This child is your bastard. You need to take care of him and responsibility for him. He's seven and driving me crazy."

"Come in, Tamsin. How can I help?"

"Give me money to take care of Graham or I'll tell your wife all about us."

"I'll tell her myself if it comes to that. She knows all my secrets. We don't like blackmail, it's a crime and no foundation for charity."

"Have it your own way. I need money and you have some responsibility for Graham."

Tim looked at Tamsin and wondered how he could have fallen for this woman years ago. He had been a corporal in the Royal Cornish Fusiliers when the affair began. No doubt he had too much to drink and fell for Tamsin's feminine charms. She had been quite fun back then but had not aged well.

She looked bedraggled and rather dirty. Her clothes were old and cheap, and she smelled of fags. Greasy hair hung down each side of her thin face. Her expression was sour and angry. What was Tim to do with her?

He explained that they were about to go on holiday and asked Tamsin to come back in six days' time. He would do what he could to help her even though he very much doubted that Graham was his son. She grudgingly accepted what he told her and left with a hostile glare and some muttered curses.

"Don't worry Tim, I'll be back. I'll stick to you like shit to a blanket. You owe me big time!"

"And I'll talk to Elizabeth. We'll see what we can do, you can count on that. May God's blessing rest upon you."

At this blessing, Tamsin glared and growled before walking off to catch the bus back to St Austell.

In the car, on the A30 well past the Welcome Home Clump, Tim told Elizabeth the whole story.

"Poor Tim. Sometimes the past comes back to bite you. We'll see how we can help."

"It came back to bite me in the arse. We did have an affair all those years ago, but I'm pretty sure that I am not Graham's father. I might have been somewhat promiscuous back then, but I did take the necessary precautions. Thank God I'm now past all that sort of thing."

"We won't let it spoil our holiday. I think this woman's trying to blackmail you. We will sort her out when we get back."

"Dear Liz. Thank you for being so understanding. I'll never stop loving you."

The holiday was a great success despite the slight cloud hanging over the couple. They stayed at Llantony near the ruins of the abbey despoiled by Henry VIII and his horrible minions. They walked up into the hills to visit the grave of Father Ignatius, the bogus mad priest, at Capel y Ffin. It was a haunted place with a strange atmosphere. And they ended up in Hay on Wye where they bought far too many books at the numerous and wonderful second-hand bookshops.

Tim was frequently startled by what he thought were glimpses of a mysterious woman who resembled Tamsin. He would half notice her for a second. Putting it down to overwork and too much imagination, he put her out of his mind.

They drove home through the mountains and over the Severn Bridge, refreshed by their break from routine. After the endless M5 and A30, they crossed the Tamar at Lanson and were soon crossing Bodmin Moor before turning north towards the shining ribbon of the sea.

It was good to return home with the prospect of a weekend clear of work until Monday. Of course, Tim took the Sunday service as usual. A priest doesn't stop saying the offices or praying to God.

He was rather thrown by seeing Tamsin and Graham sitting in the back row of benches in the nave. She made a mocking little wave as Tim stood in the pulpit to preach. He didn't let her put him off and was surprised to see that she and her son had slipped out before the end of the service. But had he really seen her again?

After the service, Tim asked various members of the congregation if they had seen the woman in the pink coat with the small boy sitting at the back of the church.

"No, us didn't see anybody apart from the usual," said Rose the postman's wife.

"There were no extra people in church this morning," said Ron Penhale, the younger churchwarden.

"I would certainly have noticed a strange young woman in the church," said bachelor farmer Phil Jasper.

So Tim had to admit that he had started seeing things, hallucinating because of the situation that was on his mind. However, he did expect Tamsin to drag her way to his door soon.

That night there was a series of thunderous knocks on the vicarage front door. Tom made his way down the stairs with a bayonet in his hand. Was the army here to claim it back? He opened the door to find the doorstep quite empty. What on earth was going on? Was he being haunted by a person who was still living? It was quite possible. The Society for Psychical Research had done a survey during the 1870s and concluded that most ghosts seen were of living people. They published the results as a book called 'Phantasms of the Living'.

The knocks continued for the next two nights with the same results. Tim knew he had to seek help once again. So, in the absence of his friend Frank who was now working most of the time at Truro Cathedral, he phoned Florence Pelleymounter.

"Hello, Tim, do come round. You're always welcome."

Sitting in front of the Aga, which was mercifully not burning, Tim explained the whole situation with no holds barred.

"It could happen to any of us. It could certainly happen to me, but we won't go there. I think that Tamsin, if she is real, is trying to take advantage of you in the same way that she might have done several years ago. If she isn't real, then we have much more and less of a problem. I'll do some research into this lass."

"Thank you, Florence. It's all a bit Thomas Hardy, isn't it?"

"Well Tim, you do surprise me. I didn't know you read Hardy."

"You'd be surprised what senior NCOs do with their spare time in hot, dusty countries when they're not trying to stay alive."

"I take that as a sign of your developing maturity," Florence said with a wicked grin.

A couple of days later Florence, true to her word, phoned Tim in the evening. He picked up the phone with a glance at Elizabeth, encouraging her to listen.

"Tim, I have some news for you. Tamsin Murphy is a real person, or I should say, was. Two years ago she threw herself and her infant son under a bus in Plymouth. Both died instantly, as did the bus driver when his vehicle swerved into a bridge.

"The Western Morning News has an interview with the boy's father, Tamsin's estranged partner. So you're off the hook. But why would she have haunted you?

"I think you'll be alright. The strength of the haunting is diminishing. It started as a complete manifestation: visual and aural, then just visual, then just aural. You may continue to see glimpses, insubstantial images from time to time. The opportunity for real harm is past."

"Thank heavens for that! Thank you, Florence. How are the lay preacher studies going?"

"Well, thank you."

"The way things are happening you'll soon be taking over the Deliverance side of my ministry. Thank you for your help."

Tim only saw Tamsin once more. Her wraith, now transparent, stood at the bus stop looking at him. Just before she melted into the background she gave a mocking little wave, as if to say: 'It was worth a try...'

Crockadon Hall

Summer in Goonperran was usually delightful. This year it was hot, sultry, and airless. 'Dead air' was muttered by more than one villager too hot to say it out loud. The wind that usually blew into the village from all four quarters had died down weeks ago. Dust lay on everything, even the dogs that slept on the road.

Revd. Tim was not put off by the airless heat. He had fought in Iraq and Afghanistan and had become somewhat used to it. But Elizabeth struggled to summon up the energy to do much except work at the primary school. She felt listless and quite unlike herself.

"Saps your strength, this does," said Ernie in the post office and village shop. "'Tis altogether too much..." Tim had to agree. His clothes were dusty and sweaty, even though they were clean that morning. He was due up to Crockadon Hall that evening to visit the couple who had recently moved there. It was a long walk uphill to the Hall so Tim decided to drive up in his ancient and battered Land Rover.

The Hall interested him. It had an old chapel attached, a long, low building that was still consecrated. The ancient family that had lived there for centuries had finally died out and the Hall had been sold to a couple from Somerset who had moved in and enthusiastically started to restore it. Tim wanted to know what would happen to the old chapel. It would be useful for occasional services for the folk who lived up around the edge of the moor, people who were still parishioners but had no links with the village.

Crockadon Hall was long and low, like the adjoining chapel. Bent trees lay behind and to the side, offering some meagre shelter from the gales that now seemed history. Behind lay the granite spine of Cornwall, rocks, tors and shaggy grass, furze and heather. On the skyline were three conical bumps, Iron Age tumuli. The view to the north was breathtaking with the sea twinkling in the far distance. But the higher altitude didn't diminish the heat radiating from a brassy sky.

"Ah, Vicar, welcome! Come in and have some lemonade." Tim was greeted by a young man in filthy jeans and a torn work shirt. "Call me Simon. And this is my wife Anna."

There was something familiar about his pretty wife, but not from a past dalliance, thought Tim.

He noticed that she wore a bandage around her neck and wondered why. None of his business of course. But he was intrigued nonetheless. Simon and Anna showed him around the rambling granite house. Low ceilings and thick walls made the interior cooler than the outside and would hold the warmth in the winter. The restoration was tasteful and well done. Tim could tell that the owners knew a lot about historic architecture. They had skimped on nothing: lime mortar and plaster, handmade glass, proper oak beams.

"I know what you're thinking," said Simon with a smile. "We're not doing the old place up for a quick sale. We want to live here and start a family and see them grow up here. I can run my architectural business from here and Anna can write articles about the restoration progress as well as the novel she has been planning for months."

After being shown around the whole property, including the chapel, Simon sat Tim down with a glass of beer. He agreed to the occasional use of the chapel and mentioned that there was a family burial ground attached. It was abandoned and overgrown; they were planning to clear it and tidy it up.

Round the back of the house Tim was surprised to see a broken pane in one of the ground floor windows. He didn't mention it and reckoned it would soon be fixed. He was most interested in the house and the chapel and looked forward to a return visit. He liked the couple who owned the place and considered them an asset to the parish.

It was quite late when he fired up his old Land Rover and drove slowly down the drive to the lane. He heard the dry rushing of wings and saw what appeared to be a large bird swooping down from the moor's edge towards the village. It was huge and Tim thought at first that it must have been an owl before remembering that owls made no noise when they flew. It diminished in size as it glided down the hill towards the village as the ground darkened and the heat diminished slightly.

When Tim returned home Elizabeth came out to meet him. She held her hand against her neck and seemed tired.

"What's the matter?" asked Tim.

"I fell asleep in the downstairs study and an insect must have come in and bitten my neck."

Tim looked carefully and noticed two marks on her neck, almost punctures. He fetched some iodine and a soft bandage and gently treated the wound.

"That's better; thanks, Tim. I do feel tired so I'll go to bed now."

When Tim went to draw the study curtains he noticed that one of the small diamond panes was broken. Shards of thin glass lay on the window sill. 'Perhaps something flew into the window when Liz was asleep and some of the glass cut her neck. How strange...'

Next day, Elizabeth felt unwell and reluctantly took the day off school. She felt terrible doing this. Tim suggested that she lie down in the study where it was marginally cooler than anywhere else. She reluctantly agreed and Tim left her with her marking and a good book.

In the afternoon, Tim answered his phone. It was Elizabeth, unusually calling him home. She said that something was scrabbling at the window trying to get in. Tim returned home straightaway and went into the study. Elizabeth looked very pale and the bandage had gone from her throat. The puncture wounds were deeper and fresher.

After taking care of his wife and getting her to move to another room, Tim examined the diamond pane window. Another pane was broken and there were deep scratches on the paint on the outside of the frame. He rushed to the phone.

"Hello, Simon? Tim here. Tell me, how's Anna today?"

"Why do you ask? Actually, she's not too good. She's very pale and sleeps a lot. The marks on her neck seem to be worse."

"Please listen carefully, Simon. It's most important that you move her upstairs and keep an eye on her. I'll be right over to explain."

Before he left, he phoned Florence Pelleymounter and asked her to come over and stay with Elizabeth. She understood at once and came straight over with her black leather bag. Tim explained what he thought was happening and where he was going and why. He was relieved to have a woman of Florence's intelligence and experience to keep an eye on his wife.

Tim accelerated the Land Rover up the long hill, foul exhaust belching out behind him. He arrived at Crockadon Hall and ran straight in through the front door.

"Simon, Anna. It's me. Is everything alright?"

"I think so," Simon replied. He was up with Anna in the master bedroom. Tim was relieved that she looked better, less pale than before.

"Has the old burial ground behind the chapel been much disturbed lately," Tim asked.

"Why do you ask? Come to think of it we did clear away some of the weeds and we found a sort of mausoleum which must have been the family tomb of the Polgrean family at one time."

"Did you go into it?"

"No, we opened the door a crack and looked in at the coffins stacked there. Some of them had fallen and spilled bones onto the floor. We decided to deal with that another day."

"Very sensible. I think we have an infestation here of a demon looking for sustenance. Both Anna and Liz have been targeted. Popular culture would call this a vampire. And, yes, I firmly believe that such things exist. I think I saw the thing flying down to the village last night. The answer doesn't lie in garlic and silver bullets but in prayer and other forms of positive action. Do not leave Anna unattended at any time. I think I can help you, but it isn't going to be pleasant. We shall need strong nerves and stomachs to solve this problem."

When Tim arrived home he was tired from constant movement up and down the hill. The heat was still oppressive and all the windows had to remain closed, both at Crockadon Hall and the vicarage. As dusk drew down Tim summoned Elizabeth and Florence to prayer. He exhorted the sinister creature to stay away and to depart to where God, in His mercy, could take care of it. He prayed for strength and resolution as well as for God's blessing on both affected families. He asked Florence to stay with Elizabeth.

A crash from downstairs interrupted the conversation. Tim ran downstairs and pulled back the study curtains. A scaly claw reached through the broken pain; two red eyes glared through the window. Tim shouted "Begone!" and the claw slid back through the splintered glass. A hunched figure outside ran in bounding steps over the lawn and took off into the evening sky. Huge leathery wings flapped and lifted the vampire above the hedge and over the churchyard.

Tim saw it turn in a northerly direction towards the moor. He reached into his desk and took out a Smith and Wesson revolver (courtesy of the British Army!). Taking a box of cartridges he left the house and jumped into the Land Rover. Another tedious drive uphill, and he arrived once more at Crockadon Hall. He knocked hard on the door and was let in.

Tim, Simon and Anna prayed the same prayers for safety and deliverance in the downstairs study. They then waited in silence. Soon heavy wing beats could be heard approaching the house and a thump on the ground outside the window confirmed the presence of the vampire.

Tim loaded his pistol and waited for the scratching at the window. It soon started.

Vampires are incredibly stupid, or just plain greedy, Tim thought as he waited with the others. Then the thin glass smashed and a heavy body started to climb through the window. Tim pulled back the curtain with his left hand and fired his pistol with the other.

There was a shrill scream and the beast withdrew. Tim saw a lumpish figure hop across the lawn in an ungainly way and vanish into the shrubbery. He heard a crash as it fell over the wall into the burial plot.

"We must stay here until it is light. It could have set a trap. If we go after it, tonight, it could grab one of us. Tomorrow we will find it and destroy it. We will have one person on guard while the others sleep. Stay together in the same room and we'll be safe."

After a restless hot night the sun came up very early and Tim, Simon and Anna left the house together to follow the trail of blood spatters over the lawn, through the bushes, and into the cemetery. A trail of flattened grass and weeds showed where the creature had dragged its crippled body over to the mausoleum of the Polgrean family.

The door, down five chipped steps, lay open. Tim led the others into the crypt, where coffins lay scattered. Stepping over numerous bones Tim saw an open coffin at the back of the chamber. He approached it carefully.

Inside lay the withered and decayed body of what had once been a man. Papery yellow skin was stretched over collapsing bone. The rib cage arched upwards above the shrivelled stomach. Thin bowed legs lay below the knobs of the pelvis. Tim was drawn to the head, just a skull really, with flaking skin stretched over prominent cheekbones. The eyes were quite gone. Pools of darkness lay on either side of the cavity that had once been a nose. But the mouth, with its withered lips, barely covered the tips of two sharp teeth from which dried blood crusted.

The other place crusted with dry blood was on the corpse's right leg. A neat bullet hole drilled the parchment skin.

"Now, we're about to do something we must never refer to again or tell anyone we have done. Will you help me move this horrible old bugger out into the burial ground? He can't hurt us now, but we must make sure that all trace of him is erased."

Tim and Simon gritted their teeth and lifted the body out of its coffin. It weighed next to nothing and made no sound apart from a dry crackling. They carried it out into the open air and laid it down on the weedy ground.

"We must make a pile of brushwood and dry twigs in the middle of the burial plot and put this old codger on top."

This was soon done and a match was put to the bottom of the pile. The flames leapt high and soon the dry corpse was surrounded by fire. It curled in the heat before blazing upwards. A dry croak was all that could be heard. When the flames died down, Tim stirred the embers with a stick to make sure that nothing was left of the remains of Matthew Polgrean, who died in 1768. A rake was found to smooth out the ashes and prayers were said.

Simon and Anna thanked Tim profusely before he left. He felt anxious as the Land Rover creaked its way back down to the village in the gathering dusk. He need not have worried; Elizabeth was feeling very much better and had enjoyed Florence's company. The two women listened while Tim explained what had happened.

"Aha!" said Florence. "This could have happened before. I remember reading a story told by a man named Augustus Hare in the 1870s. He used to entertain friends by telling spooky stories, in fact, he literally dined out on them for years.

"He told of a vampire at Croglin Grange in Cumbria that attacked a woman in a downstairs room. On trying again, it was shot by the woman's brother and hobbled back to the family crypt in a nearby burial ground. Next day, a shrivelled corpse was found with a fresh wound in its leg. It was then taken out and burned.

"On later investigation, it was found that there was no Croglin Grange, but two Croglin Halls, High and Low. The Low Hall had a blocked-up window hung about with horseshoes for good luck. So there was some truth in the story—perhaps!"

It was Elizabeth who had the last word:

"In this way does life imitate art!"

The White Bird

The summer heat had broken at last with thunderheads advancing from the west along with gusty winds. A huge drop spattered in the dust before the downfall began. Thunder pealed overhead like huge granite balls rolling in the attic of heaven.

Revd. Tim and Elizabeth were relieved that the hot weather had passed. They both felt tired from the recent alarming episode of the vampire and looked forward to life settling down at last. There was more than enough to do in three rural parishes and a lively primary school.

Since the death of Sal Scratch, more properly Sally Screech, a new witch had taken over in Goonperran. Her name was Sarah Polgooth; she was much younger than Sal and much kinder. She claimed that she was a white witch. Above her house was a weather vane in the form of a goose, a pun on Sarah's surname. She was polite and pleasant and Tim got on well with her.

Next door to Sarah lived Bert Oxenham. He was a sprightly man in his early eighties who lived alone and had done since his wife had died tragically young. He had never remarried and had never found anyone to match his late wife. So he lived quite contented into a long retirement. He was an educated man who had run a caravan park at Mother

Arscott's Bay further up the coast. His hobbies included reading, walking, and genealogy. Tim always enjoyed visiting him and having a yarn.

Bert would walk a good five miles every day, with his hazel thumb stick and old army beret. He was well known along the coast path and up on the moor. Every Christmas Day he would climb Roughtor and Brown Willy, whatever the weather. His son Arthur and his wife would often walk with him before the Christmas lunch back in Bert's snug cottage.

His genealogical research had turned up some strange facts. The Oxenham family had been living in Devon for centuries and had a secret.

"I'll tell you what it is when the time comes," Bert had cryptically told Tim on more than one occasion.

One summer evening, Bert had not returned home in time for tea. Tim was worried and set off along the coast path to try and find him. He walked over two miles before finding Bert sitting despondently on a seat overlooking the sea.

"Bert! There you are. You had us worried. Are you alright?"

Tim sat down on the seat. He found that Bert was perspiring and clammy despite the warm summer sun.

"When you're ready to go I'll walk back with you. We can take our time. I'll make sure you get home safe. We can make you some tea at the vicarage and send it over if you like."

"Thank you, Tim. I don't know what came over me. It's like a dark cloud. I'm usually pretty fit."

"That's true, but we all have our off days. Let's sit here a while."

A few quiet minutes later Bert said:

"Time to be off. Thank you for walking with me, it's a great reassurance."

He struggled to get up, leaning on his stick. "Bugger!" he said quietly. Tim had never heard him swear before so was prepared to take his condition seriously. The two men set off slowly. Bert wheezed up the hills but made valiant efforts to keep going. At Tim's suggestion, they sat down at every seat on the way and rested.

Eventually, they arrived at Bert's cottage. Tim made a pot of tea. Bert looked at him gravely and said: "Soon we'll find out if there's any substance in the family legend. But I'm not ready yet to tell you about it. I'm quite superstitious and if I mention it, it might come about."

"That's fine. I'll bring over some tea in half an hour or so."

"Many thanks, Tim. I'm going up to my room to lie down for a bit. Take your time over tea."

Tim was surprised to hear Bert's bedroom window clap closed on such a warm evening. He walked thoughtfully home.

An hour later he brought Bert's tea on a tray with a cloth over it. Elizabeth had helped make it, and it smelled appetising. He walked up to Bert's door and called up the stairs. Hearing no reply he put the tray down and walked up the stairs. Standing outside the bedroom door he heard fluttering. He opened the door to find Bert staring at a white dove circling the room over his head.

He walked into the room and opened the window to let the dove out. It flew straight out into the garden. Bert looked stricken.

"Hello, Bert. I've brought you your tea. I'll bring it up to you."

Bert nodded his thanks. After Tim had put the tray on his bed, Bert said: "Tim, I think that now is the time to tell you the family secret. That dove is the White Bird of the Oxenhams. It's like a banshee but a silent one. Before a member of the family dies, the bird is seen three times in the room.

"I've seen it once. But the chances are that I will see it twice more in the next few days. Then I shall die."

Tim looked at Bert.

"Perhaps not. You actually look much better. Perhaps you won't see the white bird for a long time."

"I hope you're right. We'll see. Many thanks to you and Elizabeth for the delicious tea."

Tim thoughtfully took his leave, leaving the old man to rest and read his library book. He walked home thinking about the power of auto-suggestion. When he mentioned it to Elizabeth, she looked up from her lesson preparation and said: "But how did the dove get into the bedroom when both the window and the door were closed?"

"Good question, I've no idea..."

A couple of days passed. Tim looked in on Bert once a day and was pleased to see him getting progressively better. On the third day, however, he found Bert looking bruised and battered sitting in his chair in the front room.

"I took a tumble down the blessed stairs, I'm afraid. Came over feeling dizzy. I'm due at the doctor's this evening so that will sort me out.

"I'm afraid I saw the bird again when I was lying on the floor at the foot of the stairs. One to go, I suppose. I think I ought to make a confession soon before it's too late."

"We can certainly do that. It needn't be in church."

So Bert recounted to Tim all the things in his life that he was less than proud of. There was nothing terrible and Tim absolved him easily.

"Now I'm ready to meet my maker."

"Don't count on it. By that, I mean that you are not necessarily on the point of death. Let's see what Dr Couch has to say this evening."

A few more busy days went by before Tim was summoned to Bert's house by a phone call. He arrived straight away to find Bert in bed looking pale and resigned.

"Has that wretched bird shown up again?"

"Not yet, but I feel it approaching closer all the time. Dr Couch sent me for tests at Bodmin General and the result is a diagnosis of congestive heart failure. The darn thing's worn out. I'm ready to go and be with my beloved Helen again after all these years. In fact, I'm looking forward to it. Thank you for all you've done for me, Tim."

Then the two men prayed together until a fluttering sound disturbed their concentration. Even though the window was shut a white dove gradually appeared and flew in circles above Bert's head. Tim moved to open the window and, as he did so, he heard a sigh coming from the bed. He turned to see Bert lying peacefully with his eyes shut and a slight smile on his lips. He was quite dead.

The funeral was attended by nearly everyone in the parish. Bert had been well-liked, and everyone was sad to see him gone. His son and daughter-in-law inherited the cottage and moved in permanently.

One of the conditions of Bert's will was a curious one. He insisted that, on his gravestone in the churchyard, there should be a carving in the slate of a white dove flying.

Wrecked!

September in Goonperran was unpredictable; gales and sunny spells, rain and lengthening shadows. At least, the heat that dominated the earlier summer months had dispersed. Revd. Tim found much more energy to go about his parish duties and was glad of it.

One afternoon, while working on his sermon, he had an unexpected visitor. He opened the door to Canon William Manhire, the Archdeacon of Bodmin.

"Nice to see you, Bill. What can I do for you?"

Tim sat Bill Manhire, known irreverently and most inaccurately as 'Rent Boy', down in the study by the open window with views of the lawn and the vegetable garden.

"Well, Tim, I've come to confirm your appointment as deliverance priest. No extra money, I'm afraid, a bit like becoming rural dean. It's a good appointment, in my opinion. You act as a magnet for paranormal incidents and have been very good at laying ghosts to rest and overcoming demons.

"Also, I would like to ask you to take on one extra parish. I wouldn't be asking you if I thought you wouldn't be up to the task. Again, no extra money, but there is the possibility of a curate for at least two years to help out. What do you say?"

"I say yes. I didn't come here looking for an easy life and God certainly seems to pile on the work, but I'll do my best."

"You haven't asked me what parish it is."

"I think I know! It has to be Trejago, shrouded in mist and superstition, one of the highest parishes in the Duchy and one of the most isolated. I'll take it on, sure enough."

"Splendid Tim, I thought you might. Don't do anything until it had been confirmed by the bishop. Nothing will happen for a few months. You may pay the place a visit but don't breathe a word to anyone about the possibility of becoming their vicar."

"Certainly not. I need a bit of breathing space and time to think about how I shall approach the parish in any case."

When Bill Manhire had left Tim walked over to the church to think about the new challenges. He decided that, yes, he really was up for them.

That evening he and Elizabeth took the time for a long walk along the cliffs. As the sun went down the wind dropped, only to swing around and blow hard from the shining sea. The coast path undulated steeply down the coombes and up onto the headlands. Ahead of them, there was a very welcome wooden bench on the cliff's top. Quite out of breath Tim and Elizabeth sank gratefully down onto it. The sun was beginning to sink into the western horizon, making a long shining sea lane reaching the bottom of the cliff.

A sailing ship was making its way up the coast quite close to the shore.

"I hope they know what they're doing," Liz murmured as she concentrated on the ship's progress. It was a fine sight, a four master with a lot of sail on view. It seemed to wallow as it dipped into the troughs between the waves of the rising sea. The crew could be seen taking in sail and scurrying about like ants on the heaving decks.

Despite the crew's best efforts the ship was fighting a losing battle. It was being drawn nearer to the rugged shore and seemed powerless to turn about and sail further out into the channel.

Tim realised that both Elizabeth and he had left their phones at home. They could only watch, horrified, as the huge ship hit the rocks under the towering cliffs. There was a faint grinding sound and shrill cries as the ship rode over the Manacles, sharp rocks that were ripping the bottom out of the hull. The whole ship rose and turned as masts crashed down onto the decks in a tangle of spars and rigging. Crates, barrels, and what appeared to be men were washed overboard into the smashing foam and breaking billows.

The whole hull was exposed lying on its side under the cliff, rocking ponderously, pivoting on the rocks. Tiny human figures were washed from the decks and broken masts and swept overboard into the roiling sea. With a great grinding crash, the ship was washed free of the rocks and foundered in deeper water. Soon only the ends of some of the spars were visible.

"We must help them," Tim called out. "Down to the beach!"

Once down the steep path, the couple were horrified to see the debris of the wreck so quickly cast ashore. Bodies were surrounded by splintered wood, boxes, and timber of every description. Nothing was left whole by the crashing waves of the hungry sea. Most of the bodies lacked limbs or heads. Sometimes just a torso could be seen coming in on a wave.

The corpses seemed to be dressed in clothes of a bygone era: striped shirts, short jackets and stocking caps.

"Was this a sail training ship, do you think?" Elizabeth asked as Tim held her steady with his arm around her.

"I don't know, but it seems that there's nobody left alive."

A large piece of timber was cast up on the strand just ahead of them. It bore the carved name 'Fille de Joie, Saint Malo'.

Tim looked even more mystified. "Just a minute! This isn't happening..." As he said those words the scene in front of them began to change. The boxes, corpses and wrack on the strand line started to fade. The hulk wallowing off the rocks faded away... The sea began to calm and the wind suddenly dropped.

"Did we really see that?" asked Elizabeth.

"Yes, we did, but not in our time. The wreck of the Fille de Joie, a French ship out of St Malo, actually happened in September 1828. It was a wild evening and the ship went down with all hands. We've just seen it happen again. But why?"

There was nothing more to see except the red orb of the sun sinking beneath the calm sea. Mystified, Tim and Elizabeth headed home, determined not to talk about it.

It took a few days to get over what they had seen, but soon Tim and Elizabeth were as busy as ever. One afternoon, Tim went over to see his trainee lay reader Florence Pelleymounter. He told her what he had seen on the clifftop that evening.

"Most interesting," said Florence thoughtfully. "We've all heard of the wreck of the Fille de Joie. It's famous. But why it should happen again for just an audience of two is a complete mystery. Mind you, it could be a warning. There could be another wreck along this coast in the next few weeks."

"I can hardly go to the Coastguards and say that a wreck is about to happen. And that I know because Liz and I saw a vision. They'd consider me as mad as a kipper."

"True enough. Next time you walk on the cliffs for heaven's sake, take your phone. And pray about it. You have been chosen to experience the portent. There must be a reason behind it all."

"I'll wait until the weather conditions are similar to how they were the other evening and I'll set out along the cliff."

The days passed in a whirl of services, meetings, visits to parishioners, and the minutiae of parish life. Tim forgot about his vision on the cliffs, just as he forgot about the forthcoming new extra parish of Trejago. He hardly had a day off, hardly had time to tend the vegetable garden or stroke Crowley, his huge black cat. But he had time for prayer and contemplation and lots of time for Elizabeth. He considered any neglect of her to be a mortal sin!

One sultry evening, he had a feeling that he should be up on the cliffs. Elizabeth insisted on coming too. Tim was glad because she gave him strength, and her witness would show him that he was not hallucinating or going mad. When he was younger, he might have led a wild life, but he never took drugs, even though they were often available. They would reduce his effectiveness as a soldier and affect his judgement. That was one thing at least that he got right. So, no flashbacks...

They took binoculars (which never made it back to QM's stores when Tim left the army) and some flares. Also a camera and a first aid kit. They walked thoughtfully along the cliffs until, at last, they came to the bench high on the cliff. They sat down, now convinced that nothing was going to happen.

After a few minutes, the weather began to change. Clouds obscured the sun and the sea rose. A strong, gusty wind began to blow on shore. A tramp steamer approached from the west. It was black with long streaks of rust streaking the hull. Wallowing from side to side it grew larger as it approached the rocky shore.

"Turn to port," Elizabeth hissed between clenched jaws. The ship took no notice but continued its relentless wallow towards the cliff.

"For Pete's sake, Turn!" Tim shouted. Obviously, the crew on the ship couldn't hear him. Then Tim remembered the flares. He stood on the cliff's edge and lit the first one. It shot out a bright red flare which arced over the ship and exploded with a loud crack right above it. Tim fired two more, with the same result.

Then, gradually the ship began to turn. Little by little it turned away from the high cliffs and jagged rocks of the barren shore. Tim and Elizabeth saw a flare shoot up from the bridge acknowledging the signals. As the ship turned away, now safe from the rocks, Tim lifted up the binoculars to his eyes. He focussed on the blunt stern.

He was just able to make out the ship's name, streaked like everything else on the vessel with rust. The raised painted letters read: FILLE DE JOIE, PANAMA.

"Do not mention this to anyone except Florence," Tim insisted. "Those flares I fired were illegal. They were out-of-date distress flares that I found in the shed. I could get in a lot of trouble if anyone found out what I did."

Relieved that the lifeboat had not been called out in response to the three flares, Tim and Elizabeth set off for home and a late supper of pasties that were warming up in the over.

"I still don't believe in an interventionist God," Elizabeth remarked. "I don't think we can bully God into changing things."

"I quite agree. In this case, we were given God's grace to do something, to prevent a tragedy. The watch officers must have been watching a football match on the television. They were negligent and must have learned a lesson. I'm sure they won't report the flares just as we won't report the near miss with the rocks."

After the warm pasty supper and a cup of strong tea, Tim said to Elizabeth:

"It's Saturday tomorrow. Why don't we go and have a look at Trejago?"

At that moment the phone rang. Tim picked it up.

"Hello, Tim here."

"Hello, this is Bill Manhire. I'd like you to meet your new curate tomorrow. Do you fancy a morning in Trejago? I think you'll like her. She's from Devon, but don't hold that against her. I think she'll do very well. She's from the country and should settle well here. What do you think?"

"Great, we'll meet you there at ten o'clock. It's true to say that God moves in mysterious ways…"

Trejago

The autumn musts were gathering up on the moor as Revd. Tim set out in his extraordinarily disreputable Land Rover to meet his new curate in the remote moorland parish of Trejago. He was amused by the reputation of the place: a small village clustered around the church with hunched buildings sheltered by high granite hedges.

Labouring up the last hill Tim saw the village in front of him through the mizzle. The sign announcing 'Trejago' had been graffitied with the words' Villige of the dammed'. Either it was true or some wag had tried to cheer it up. The road was muddy and full of potholes. It took Tim to the desolate treeless square surrounded by sullen low houses. Some were Cornish Units with mansard roofs, others square semis built from mundic.

Trejago was obviously a mining village which had become moribund when the tin and copper mines closed. Even the arsenic here was worked out. What people did for a living Tim had no idea. It made Princetown, on Dartmoor, look like the French Riviera.

At least it had a shop and post office with a small draughty cafe attached to the back. Sitting at one of the tables, still wearing her coat, was a jolly-looking grey-haired woman who greeted Tim enthusiastically:

"Hello! You must be Revd. Tim. I'm Pat, your new curate. I'm very pleased to meet you."

Tim replied with similar enthusiasm. He liked the look of this middle-aged lady who exuded confidence and capability.

He ordered coffee from the rather sour-faced woman who ran the shop. It arrived in chipped mugs with faded photos of Prince Charles and Lady Diana on their sides.

"What is it about this place?" quietly asked Pat. "It seems to have a down on itself."

"I don't know. But I intend to find out."

Pat Pearce was a Devon woman from Foghanger, near Tavistock. She had worked as a social worker in Plymouth before being called to the ministry. She was glad to get out of the city. Her husband had been stabbed to death years before while walking down Union Street one morning. A deranged man had rushed out of Diamond Lil's and stuck a knife in him while saying 'Good Morning'.

She had remained happily single bringing up her son and had taken early retirement before going to theological college in Exeter. So here she was in one of the highest and dreariest villages in Cornwall, at the heart of the bleak granite interior. She wondered if becoming a missionary would be easier. Hot countries had always appealed to her.

The coffee was cold and, frankly, rather dreadful. They were glad they had not tried the heavy cakes that appeared to be made of cement dust and mundic. Of course, they were too polite to say so.

They wrapped up warm to walk around the village. Everything was bleak and grey. There were signs of deprivation and desperation everywhere. Several houses had brooms standing with the bristles upmost.

"Do you know what that means?" Tim asked.

"No idea," Pat replied.

"It means that the single woman who lives in that house is looking for a man. Like army wives putting an OMO packet in the window, indicating 'on my own'."

He expected Pat to be shocked. He was glad when she took it in her stride, a good indication of her suitability as a curate.

"I promise you I won't be doing that," she added.

They came to the low, grey church which had ferns growing out of the walls and a small tree sprouting from the tower. They tried to open the door but found it firmly locked. They went back to the shop to try to find out who held the key.

"That'll be the churchwarden, Mr Crago. There's not much call for the church to be open these days."

"Really??" Tim's eyebrows shot skyward.

Mr Crago opened the door of his dingy house. When he saw Tim's clerical collar, he fetched the church key without a word. Handing it over ne said:

"Nobody goes into the church anymore since the village was cursed. There seems no point..."

"By the way, I'm your new vicar. My name's Tim, and this is my new curate Pat."

"'Ess. Good luck to you both." And Mr Crago firmly shut his front door.

"If that's the churchwarden, I wonder what the rest of the flock are like."

"Like the village, heavy weather, I think. It's definitely going to be a challenge."

The rusty key turned harshly in the old lock. Tim had to put his shoulder to the oak door to open it. Then they stepped down into the nave of the church. It had once been a fine building but had obviously fallen on hard times. The windows were streaked with cobwebs and filth; mould covered whole sections of the wall; the hymnbooks were damp. The inside of the church radiated a chill that was more than the low temperature. Even the slate slabbed floor felt damp. Plaster was flaking off the damp walls.

"The house of God needs our attention," said Pat.

"And people to fill it," added Tim.

They walked up the nave and down the aisles. Beyond the screen, the sanctuary felt high and remote. A treacly stained glass window festooned with cobwebs let in little light and the tattered altar frontal did little to enhance the sanctuary.

Walking back to the nave through the screen door Tim noticed a very dilapidated monument in the north aisle. It was the only family monument in the church. It dated from the early eighteenth century and depicted skulls and broken columns as well as the bewigged figure of a thin recumbent gentleman. Although lying down he seemed restless and ready to twist himself into a standing position. His thin face held a haughty sneer of boredom.

"James Hamilton, Bart." Tim remarked. "I wonder if he was the owner of the mines that once existed round here."

"Mr Crago mentioned that the village is cursed. We need to do some research on the history of this place. If there is a curse, we can surely lift it, with God's help."

"In the meantime let's go downhill to where the sun shines. We'll come back when we know more about the place."

Tim walked Pat to her car and fixed a date for a meeting at Goonperran. He said goodbye and climbed into his Land Rover with a sense of relief. His spirits rose as he drove downhill off the moor and saw the sea twinkling in the distance and the tower of his church surrounded by beech trees.

On the subject of cursed villages, a visit to Dr Pelleymounter was called for. So Tim found himself sitting comfortably in front of her Aga once more nursing a cup of tea.

"Oh yes! The curse of Trejago. When the tin, copper, and finally arsenic ran out in the parish during the 1930s, Frederick Hamilton, the last mine owner was ruined, partly by his refusal to invest in safety gear and new mining technology. He had no heirs when he died and cursed the village, the people and St James' church on his deathbed. Since then the village has never prospered. No new houses have been built. Many of the men of the parish have died young, mostly from mining diseases and later from accidents. People don't move into Trejago, even second homeowners. Nobody goes to church anymore except to be buried.

"It could all be turned around, you know. I'm sure that your taking the parish on is its last chance. The bishop doesn't want to close the church even though it hasn't paid its parochial share for decades. The last time I was there I looked at the Parochial Register. It showed just three names and someone had written 'bugger all' across it. That sums the place up at the moment."

This information gave Tim pause for thought. He had been called to reverse the historic decline of a community that had become a basket case. He went home and made a few notes in his study with Crowley, his enormous black cat, issuing rumbling purrs on his lap.

He decided to call a parish meeting in the Village Hall in Trejago. He would pin up posters and provide a supper there for anyone who chose to come. The title would be 'A New Beginning'. Pat and Elizabeth would help him, and he would put forward his ideas for putting hope and the love of God back into the community.

The day of the meeting was fine. Tim and Elizabeth drove noisily up to Trejago which, for once, wasn't shrouded in mist and drizzle. It still looked pretty grim, especially the Village Hall which was a time capsule of thirties asbestos panelling.

Once inside they put the coffee on and started to prepare lunch, hoping for someone to turn up. They were not disappointed; knots of men and women in drab clothes shuffled into the Hall and were given a cup of coffee and a saffron bun. Most then sat down rather reluctantly. At last, the hall was almost full of people and Tim began with a prayer and introductions.

"I have been asked to take over this parish with the help of Pat, my curate. I have come here not to criticise you but to help you and to work with you to make life better.

"Let's begin with the church. Who will come and help Pat, Elizabeth and me to give it a good autumn clean on Saturday? We will scrub the floor, get the mould off the walls, and wax the benches. We'll get rid of the cobwebs and tidy everything up. Has anyone here got the use of a tractor and trailer to take away the rubbish?"

Two hands went up, a very good sign.

"If you come and help us on Saturday we'll give you hot pasties and as much tea as you can drink. We'll say some prayers and the office of matins. We'll have good fun and get dirty. Uz'll 'ev a few laughs."

He didn't ask for hands up to find out who would be there. He had faith that quite a few would come, and he wasn't disappointed.

On Saturday morning, the three friends came dressed as Sal Scratch. They had on their oldest clothes. Tim wore his army lightweights (thou shall not steal!) and Elizabeth her oldest jeans. Pat wore an ancient wax jacket that undoubtedly had been pulled through a hedge backwards, many times.

"Welcome, good people of Trejago. Today we'll make God's house a fit and pleasant place for worship and fellowship. I've brought scrubbing brushes, cloths, dusters, wax, woodworm oil, and a load of other stuff. Each of you choose what you want to do and we'll make up teams. But, first, we'll say matins and pray for the parish and people of Trejago."

The day went well. Between thirty and forty men, women and children worked hard sprucing up the church. No less than two trailer loads of mouldy hassocks, rotting cassocks, old hymn books and all sorts of wreckage were taken away to be disposed of on various moorland farms. Soon the armpit smell of damp was replaced by the smell of polish and wax and soapy water.

"Splendid! Proper job! Time to stop for a bit of croust. Tiddy oggies for all and lots of tay."

He got quite a laugh for putting on a bit of Cornish. But what really brought the house down was when he said: "I apologise to all you Dolly Pentreaths here who don't speak English. Can't say I blame you!"

At the end of the afternoon, Tim said prayers of thanks to God, thanked everybody and said: "In two weeks' time we'll have a service of rededication here at 11 o'clock. We'll rid the village of its curse. I'd love as many people as possible to come. It doesn't matter if you are not a church person. St James' is here for everybody; it's your church."

As Tim and Elizabeth were leaving the church, Mr Crago came shyly up to them and asked them back to his house for the evening meal. He seemed a different person, no longer guarded and surly but open and full of hope.

The two weeks passed quickly before Tim, Elizabeth and Pat were back in St James' Church once more. The village was still grey and depressing, but St James' was spick and span and ready for the challenges ahead.

The church began to fill up with men, women and children who no longer looked drab. They were perhaps a little shabby, but they were clean and as happy as they had been on the day of the great church clean-up.

The service went well with the church almost full for the first time in many years. The organ playing was a little rusty, but the singing was wonderful in the way that only Cornish singing can be. Then came the climax of this service of rededication. Tim stood on the chancel step in the open screen doorway and prayed for the lifting of the curse. It didn't matter if it was a real curse or not, it was the perception that needed changing.

As the congregation said a loud 'Amen' a cracking sound came from the Hamilton tomb in the north aisle. Dust began to rise from the marble as it slowly shifted on its foundation. Pilasters crashed down and carved stones slipped from the top. Among the dusty haze the figure of James Hamilton, Bart. appeared to writhe and attempt to rise from its recumbent position. Then it fell with a great crash into the aisle and shattered into pieces. The rest of the monument collapsed after it burying the remains in more chunks of stone.

Fortunately, nobody was sitting near the despised monument so nobody was injured. A huge gasp went up from the congregation followed by a loud cheer.

"Great!" said Tim to no one in particular. "If that isn't a sign I don't know what is..."

School Story

Elizabeth enjoyed working as deputy head teacher at St Piran's C of E Primary School in Goonperran. It was a school for the whole area in North Cornwall and had over one hundred students from all walks of life. The last Ofsted report had classified it as outstanding, mainly due to the dedication of all the staff rather than the meagre funding it received from the Cornwall County Council Education Department. Expectations and dedication were high and education, although serious, was considered fun.

Elizabeth was glad to welcome two new girls into her Year Five class. Their names were Mary and Sophie Prout, and they were identical twins. They came from a farm down by the cliffs and had apparently moved over from another local primary school. They were short and dark with identical pudding basin fringes and plain, rather old-fashioned clothes. They didn't interact much with the other children and didn't say very much. They seemed perfectly content to inhabit their own, silent world. Maybe they were embarrassed by their pronounced Cornish accents and use of many old-fashioned phrases.

The other children welcomed them without the silly teasing that farm kids sometimes came in for. They learned to give them space and not to pester them, finding them somewhat remote and otherworldly. No moos or baas followed them around the playground.

As half term approached Elizabeth organised a school day trip to Tintagel Castle for the older children. She arranged for an educational pass with English Heritage, or English Heretics as she found herself calling the organisation. She booked the coaches from Sam Prouts (no relation to the twins as far as she could tell), organised free lunches, did the inevitable risk assessment, and wrote letters home.

The day out arrived fine and breezy. Before the trip, Elizabeth had taught the history of the legend of King Arthur and the Saxon invasion of Cornwall. She gave out worksheets that were fun and imaginative and made up a list of names, addresses and phone numbers. She noted with amusement that Mary and Sophie gave their number as Goonperran 140.

When the two coaches arrived outside the school they parked under the chestnut trees. Elizabeth and the other teachers who were going on the trip counted all the children onto the coaches, checking their names off on her list. There were thirty-seven children on the 'Queen of Cornubia' and thirty-eight on the 'Rose of Camelot'. Then she gave the order to leave.

It took about three-quarters of an hour for them to arrive in Tintagel, where the coaches laboriously turned down the steep lane to reach the car park beyond the church, which stood quite a way out of the village. She gathered the children in two groups in the churchyard, sheltering from the wind in the lee of the Cornish hedges.

"Before we set off to walk along the path to the castle and the new bridge that will take us to it I must point out that the cliffs here are very steep and dangerous. On no account, go near them or leave the path. Stick together at all times and never, ever, wander off on your own. Does everybody understand that?"

Hands shot up to show that they were listening and had understood her instructions. They set off in two crocodiles, following the high Cornish hedge with its herringbone slate walls until the church on the headland was left behind with only the top of the square tower showing above the grass and ferns of the hedges. The path led down towards the village on the other side of a narrow valley.

There, ahead of them, was the castle; a few ragged walls on a steep and rocky island, linked to the mainland by an elegant arched bridge. They clattered carefully down some steps cut in the valley's side until they came to the end of the bridge leading to the island castle. Elizabeth showed her pass to the bearded custodian, and they walked gingerly over the bridge. The incoming tide swirled beneath them and the waves crashed on the rocky cliffs of the island.

The custodian, Mr Tremain, gave them a very good tour, explaining the difference between fact and legend. The children listened well and took in all the information, asking good and intelligent questions at the end before filling in their worksheets and drawing a sketch and a diagram of the castle.

Mr Tremain was impressed and told Elizabeth and the other teachers that he had enjoyed showing them all around and answering their questions. He hoped they would all come back soon to further explore this historic and dramatic site.

After picnic lunches and a check that no litter had been left, the school party, tired but happy, walked back, a little more confidently, over the high arched bridge, climbed up the steep steps and back along the cliff path following the hedge to the church. They sat down to rest on the springy turf of the churchyard while Elizabeth carefully counted off the members of the two groups. She went through the list three times. Each time she found that there were two names missing.

She asked the other teachers: "Have you seen Mary and Sophie Prout?" No one had, and, so as not to alarm the children, she asked the coach drivers to unlock the two coaches and asked the children to get onto the coach that had brought them there.

Freddy Mitchell opened one of the coach windows from inside.

"They're here, Miss. Mary and Sophie are sitting on the back seat."

"Thank you, Freddy. I'm so glad. I can't understand how they go there, but never mind."

She climbed up into the 'Queen of Cornubia' and made her way to the back seat.

"Mary and Sophie, there you are. We couldn't find you. How did you get in?"

The twins looked blankly at her and said nothing. They looked tired and ready to go home.

"Never mind. All's well that end well."

When the bus arrived back under the chestnut trees, resplendent in their autumn colours, Elizabeth made sure that all the children had everything they had taken and that they were on the right buses to go home. She realised that she didn't know how Mary and Sophie got home. There was no one to meet them so she asked them: "How do you two usually get home?"

Mary replied: "Us walks home. Us walks everywhere. Us likes walking."

Elizabeth made a note to contact their parents to check that this was correct and said goodbye to them. They gave her a solemn look before walking off downhill towards their home.

That evening Elizabeth suggested to Tim that they walk down to the Prouts' farm on the coast. They set off after tea, Elizabeth intending to ask Mr and Mrs Prout about their daughters' arrangements for getting to and from school.

It was a glorious evening. The wind had died down and the sun hung above the western sea lanes. At last, they came to the Prouts' farm. It lay in a hollow above the cliffs and seemed deserted. As they approached there was no barking of dogs or lowing of cows.

Tim stopped in amazement. The farmhouse and the barns had no roofs. Jagged masonry pointed to the darkening sky. The gate lay on its side and the vegetable garden was a riot of brambles and small bushes. Glassless windows revealed walls devoid of plaster. Surely they must have made a mistake...

Not so. There, standing together, were the two girls, in the field beyond the ruined farm. They waved and pointed to the ground. Tim and Elizabeth waved back and walked towards them.

In the blink of an eye, they were no longer there. Tim reached the spot where they had stood. There was no disturbance in the long grass to show where they had stood. He marked the spot that they had pointed to, not quite sure why he had done that. Then, mystified, they walked away from the stick in the ground to the ruins of the farm.

"Look!" Elizabeth exclaimed. "There some sort of plaque."

On the farmyard wall facing the field in which they had seen, the girls was a tarnished plaque. Rubbing at it with his hand Tim Read aloud: "On 21 September 1943, a German bomber crashed into this farmhouse, killing Mary and Sophie Prout and the pilot Unterofficier Helmut Heuer. May They Rest in Peace."

Tim turned to Elizabeth. "Those children were telling us something. There is no German pilot buried in any of the parish cemeteries."

Next day, Tim came back with George Uren, a spade and a large, clean plastic sheet. They found the stick in the ground and started digging. The soil was dry and soon they found what they were looking for.

Among the jumble of bones, Tim picket out an Iron Cross and the remains of a leather helmet complete with a broken microphone.

"I think we've found Herr Heuer," said George.
"Yes, with a little bit of help from our friends…"

A Nice Little Girl

Revd. Tim and Elizabeth Tremaine found it hard to believe that he had been Vicar of Goonperran and three other North Cornish parishes for a year. A lot had happened in that time: they had married and settled happily down in the vicarage, another parish had been added to the team, he now had a capable curate living in a much revived Trejago, and Florence Pelleymounter had started her training for the lay ministry.

He had also become Deliverance Minister for the Deanery, not a thing to broadcast, but he was there to help with all sorts of paranormal disturbances. It would be fair to say that he had already had more than his share of psychic problems. He acted as a magnet for them, it seemed.

He wasn't surprised when, one evening, he had a phone call from Mrs Nankivell who lived with her husband and young daughter in the house formerly occupied by Sat Scratch (actually Sally Screech) the witch who had hanged herself there. The Nankivells had transformed the house from a dirty, run-down slum into a light and pleasant house which made Tim think of his parents' house in Penzance. Nevill Nankivell was a builder who specialised in the restoration of historic houses, using traditional materials and skills. Not that their ex-council house was in the least historic.

But it had responded to the right treatment and now was a lovely family home.

"Hello, Tim, I think we've got a problem here. Please could you come round soon and bless the house with holy water. There have been some funny things going on centred on Suzie. She a nice girl and all this is making her unhappy."

"Certainly Rosie, I'll come straight away. Will the whole family be there? It would be helpful if they were."

"Yes, Nev and Susie will be here with me. Many thanks. See you in a minute."

Tim organised what he would need for the blessing. He wasn't at all surprised that some residue of Sal remained. She would have been horrified by the changes in the house and garden. Hopefully, a blessing would be enough to settle her down.

He recognised the house and the effect it had on the other houses in the close. Most had been spruced up and looked like good places to live. Grey walls had been painted and gardens tidied and made productive. A proper Cornish stone hedge surrounded the Nankivells' house, replacing the wire and posts that were rusting and rotting before.

Tim knocked at the freshly painted front door which was opened immediately by Nevill. "Come in," he said. "Welcome!"

Tim walked into the kitchen as a loud crash startled him. Two smashed plates lay on the floor. He sat down on a chair.

"This sort of thing keeps happening. Crockery falls on the floor, the duvet is snatched from Suzie's bed, pictures fall, and the cat yowls at invisible things in the corners of some of the rooms. Also there is a feeling of oppression and despair in the front room and in Suzie's bedroom. It's starting to affect us and Suzie most of all."

Suzie came into the room at that point. She was a pretty little girl, very intelligent and self-possessed. She smiled at Tim and said hello. She was eight years old and doing very well in Elizabeth's class at the village primary school.

"Ah, Suzie, what have you been up to?"

"I took off all my clothes and danced around in the road with a bread knife, cutting out people's eyes."

"Suzie! You did no such thing! What on earth are you saying?"

"You're not my mother. You can't tell me what to do. Go to Hell!"

"Go to your room, Suzie. What are you saying?"

Tim noticed that she had not raised her voice, and he approved.

"You can see how this is affecting her. She's usually such a nice girl."

"And will be again, with God's help."

Tim put his stole over his shoulders and took out his bottle of holy water, box sprig and bowl. He prayed as he flicked holy water into the corners of all the rooms on the ground floor. The tabby cat fled out of an open window.

Once upstairs the process was repeated until they came to Suzie's room.

"Suzie, you can come out now if you're prepared to be nice."

"No! Shan't! Bugger off!"

"She normally never swears. She's trying to get us to react. Trying to make us angry. But we won't fall for that."

"Quite right. It's not really her who's talking. This isn't actually possession, but more influencing by something evil. I don't want to alarm you, but this is quite serious."

Nevill opened Suzie's bedroom door and, firmly but gently, picked her up and carried her downstairs. She growled and swore, using a few words that Tim never used since he left the army. He refused to be shocked, knowing that it wasn't really Suzie who was struggling, shouting, and blaspheming. She scratched her father's cheek with her long nails, drawing blood.

Her room was freezing cold when they entered. When Tim flicked the holy water, the bed rose into the air and began to sway from side to side. Chairs crashed to the floor and a complete set of Harry Potter rose into the air and fluttered about the room. But Tim carried on with the blessing and the prayers. A low, deep growling filled the room and the bedroom window cracked from top to bottom. The three adults withdrew back to the kitchen for a cup of tea and a conference.

"I'm going to have to find out what it is that's causing all of this. It isn't Suzie. She's being used as a catalyst, a vessel concentrating the evil. She's in no way responsible for what is happening. She's a very nice girl."

But when she came back into the kitchen she didn't appear to be so. She glared at everyone and ground her teeth. Her hair hung in dirty hanks down the sides of her face, and her clothes were streaked with mud.

"Sod off Prelate! Get the hell out of this house. We all hate you, you stinking hypocrite!"

Then she stamped out, heavy footsteps crashing up the stairs. They heard her bedroom door slam.

"Where did she get those words from? Prelate? We try never to swear in this house. The strongest word we use is 'fishcakes', and that is always used to make Suzie laugh. But not anymore."

Tim took his leave, promising to come back next day.

That evening he asked Elizabeth: "Suzie Nankivell; how's her work and behaviour at school at the moment?"

"Funny you should mention that. Her work's gone right off. She scrawls all over her book. Her neat handwriting is no longer used. She looks sullen and dirty, and she mutters horrible things under her breath that she thinks we can't hear. Out in the playground, she's become a bully and most unpleasant with the other children.

"I am about to talk to her parents very soon and find out what the problem is."

Tim then told her about his visit to the Nankivell's house that day and how the blessing had mainly failed. He thought that Sal Scratch was responsible for the disturbance and the changes. He had prayed about it and decided that a service of Deliverance would be necessary to solve the problem.

"Why not exorcism?" Elizabeth asked.

"It could come to that. The Deliverance would direct what's left of Sal towards God and His mercy. I have to persuade her to go to the light. Exorcism is the last resort which would send her howling into outer darkness far from God."

"I see. I do hope it works. Do you need to consult the bishop?"

"Yes, I do. And soon, before Suzie is possessed by the evil side of Sal Scratch."

Next day, Tim drove down to Truro for his appointment with Bishop Gerald.

"Ah, Tim. This sounds very serious. I think you're doing the right thing and please do the service of Deliverance. I give you my blessing and my payers. I'll ask Frank to come and help you. In this instance, two priests are better than one. There will have to be a period of fasting and prayer before you go to the Nankivells. You must let nothing distract you from the task once it has begun. Do not let any doubts or weakness affect you. The Devil will try anything to distract you from your task. But you, above all, know that."

Tim felt reassured by his talk with the bishop. He could do what he had proposed, but it would not be easy. He drove his stinking Land Rover back to Goonperran wondering, at last, if there was a diocesan grant for a decent vehicle.

The day before the Deliverance was spent in fasting and prayer: no pasties of Tinners', no baked beans or saffron cake. Frank came to the vicarage and the two men prayed together.

"Remember, Frank, that whatever comes out of Suzie's mouth did not come from her. There is nothing hateful about her. She is a very nice little girl."

Once in the Nankivells' house Tim and Frank climbed the stairs to Suzie's bedroom. Her parents remained on the landing outside. Suzie was lying on her bed staring angrily at the ceiling.

"Scum! Hypocrites! Why are you here? Get the hell out of here. I hate you both. Bunch of wankers!"

Ignoring her rants the priests began to pray aloud, consigning the demon to God's mercy. They forced themselves to ignore her shrieks and obscenities. She glared at them with black eyes, then rose slowly from her bed in a horizontal position. Smelly urine dribbled onto the bed as she gnashed her teeth.

The prayers increased. Suzie, now suspended between bed and ceiling, started to shriek and scream, shout and swear. She spat at the priests, howled like a wolf. Tim felt his powers wane. But he continued to struggle and pray aloud. At the climax of the deliverance, something remarkable happened.

Suzie fell silent and drifted down to lie on the bed. Her eyes turned red, and her mouth opened. A jet of foul black liquid shot out onto the carpet. Then, with a whimper, Suzie turned over and appeared to be asleep. Tim took her pulse. It was perfectly normal.

He turned to her parents. "She's sleeping now. We'll wait until she wakes up and take it from there."

The freezing cold had gone from the bedroom. Suzie was sleeping peacefully, breathing deeply.

Half an hour later she woke up. She called out:

"Mum?" in her normal voice. Her eyes were clear and blue once again, and she was relaxed.

"What happened?" she asked. "I must have been asleep. I had some very strange dreams about a woman in black called Sally. She's gone now, thank goodness. Oh, hello Revd. Tim. What are you doing here? It's nice to see you and your friend."

"We were here to help you get rid of your dreams. I think we succeeded. Sally will never bother you again."

And to prove the point Arlo, the huge tabby cat, came into Suzie's bedroom, purred, and rubbed himself against her leg.

Major Wylie

It would be fair to say that almost nobody in the village of Goonperran got on with Major Wylie. Even Revd. Tim honestly didn't like him although he tried to let it not show. The few exchanges he had with the good major were acrimonious. Wylie openly sneered at the church and at Tim although Tim had done absolutely nothing to offend him.

He lived in a dark old house at the western end of the village behind high walls and dense shrubs. His ex-batman from the army Sidney Bounder looked after him with grim devotion. Bounder was a wizened gnome of a man almost as old as his master and marginally more pleasant. He was devoted to Wylie in a dog-like way. The fact that Wyley was thoroughly nasty in no way detracted from his devotion.

"Percy was a fine officer," he would say to anyone who would talk to him. "Although utterly ruthless."

One evening in early autumn, Tim answered the phone with the sixth sense that someone had died. And indeed it was so; Bounder had heard a crash in the night and found Wyley at the bottom of the stairs with his head at an impossible angle.

"What's happened?" asked Elizabeth.

"The good Major's been found at the bottom of the stairs. Dead's a rag."

"May God have mercy on his soul. He won't be much missed in the village."

Tim remembered what Percy Wyley had looked like, tall and thin with greying ginger hair, a bristly moustache, bulging blue eyes and a habitual expression of distaste. He was rude and obnoxious, blunt to the point of insult. Tim wished he could think of something nice to remember him by, but even that was beyond him.

Wyley's body was taken away for autopsy. The coroner cut him open, took out his vital organs, weighed them, and sewed him back up, declaring that he had died of a broken neck with no suspicious circumstances. He released the body for burial.

No local undertaker would touch him so a firm from St Austell was asked to do the honours. Tim, of course, was to take the service and wondered how many people would be in church to see Major Wyley off. He prepared a few words of charitable, but not very accurate, things to say at the service. The sexton was to toll the bell and a grave had been dug on the north side of the churchyard.

The day of the funeral was misty and cold. A few dead leaves blew about in the square in front of the lych-gate. Slowly the hearse drew up to the lych-gate steps. The bearers got slowly out and opened the back of the hearse, sliding the coffin out and lifting it onto their shoulders. Tim, standing beside the gate in clean surplice and stole, wondered why there were four bearers instead of the usual six. They seemed rather too old for the job. Tim wondered how they were going to manage to lift the heavy casket up the steps of the lych-gate.

He didn't have to wonder for long. Half-way up the steps the leading bearer slipped on a leaf and the coffin began to tilt dangerously. The point of balance was reached, despite the best efforts of the bearers, and the coffin and its contents slipped off their shoulders, to land with a rending crash on one corner. The lid bulged open, spilling the contents onto the steps.

What landed at the bottom of the steps was not an embalmed corpse in a black suit with arms crossed on its chest and eyes and mouth sewn shut. Three granite boulders rolled into the road, leaving the red satin lining of the coffin exposed and entirely empty.

A gasp went up from the few people gathered in the square to see Major Wyley finally buried. Tim announced that the funeral was cancelled and called the police on his mobile phone. He strode back into the vestry to take off his cassock, surplice and stole. He was mystified and astounded.

When the police came Tim explained what had happened and wondered where Wyley's corpse actually was. He had never experienced anything like it before. After some silent prayers in church, he and Elizabeth returned quietly to the vicarage for a cup of tea.

They were sitting in the kitchen when the phone rang. It was Sidney Bounder.

"Vicar, I thought something like this would happen. Please come to Major Wyley's house and I'll explain. Don't talk to the police until you've heard me out."

"I'll be right there," Tim replied, mystified.

Once in Wylie's dark, secret house, he sat in the drawing room with a very agitated Sidney Bounder. At last, Bounder began to explain: "Percy Wylie was an extraordinary man. He was the illegitimate brother of Aleister Crowley and was given a new surname and identity to give him a chance in life.

"He joined the army and made a very good career. He served with distinction during the war and, as I said before, was utterly ruthless. This had its place during the war, but afterwards, in peacetime, it held him back.

"In 1940, he contacted his half-brother who was then old and sick and living in Hastings. Alistair had some secrets to tell him and some instructions. He told him that if he gave his soul to the Devil he would survive the war and live to a ripe old age. As a result Percy's life, apart from a lack of promotion beyond major, was a material success.

"What was most remarkable was what happened to him in the war at Monte Cassino in 1944. Let me show you some photographs."

He dug into his greasy leather wallet and produced three small prints. The first showed a grim-faced officer with a bristly moustache and three pips on each shoulder standing in a sunlit piazza outside a cafe.

The second showed Captain Wylie lying on his back on rocky ground. His eyes were open, and he was actually smiling. Tim could see a pair of legs lying some distance away. But what really horrified him and churned his stomach was that of Wylie's mid-section, there was just a mass of twisted entrails and slivers of white bone.

Tim looked at Wylie's face again. The man was obviously alive and uncharacteristically amused.

The third image showed a slightly older Wylie with a major's crown on his shoulders, whole and unwounded, marching along an Italian street in some sort of victory parade. Extraordinary!

"But how does that explain the rocks in the coffin?" Tim enquired.

"I really don't know. I wish I did. I shall give myself up to the police before they come looking for me. I'll try to answer their questions. I assure you that I had nothing to do with this, just as I was not responsible for what happened to him at Monte Cassino. You have to believe me. I am telling the truth."

Bounder was a greasy, weasely sort of man, but his words had the ring of truth about them. Tim had to admit that he believed him.

A few days later Sidney Bounder was released from police custody with no stain on his name. When Wylie's will was read, Bounder had left nothing at all. He didn't inherit the house or anything that had belonged to Major Wylie. Quite soon he left the village and vanished without a trace, the last victim of Major Wylie's pact with the Devil.

The body was never found. Tim wondered if it would one day be found shrivelled and desiccated, in an attic or a sea cave, but it never showed up. Elizabeth had the last word:

"They say the Devil looks after his own. Major Wylie gave the lie to this. He followed the example of Satan the Liar by providing in no way for his faithful servant."

Tim couldn't help feeling sorry for poor Bounder.

The Beast from the North

The autumn leaves were wet and mouldy. They clung to the surface of the square like dead flat fish on a quay. The wind howled around the houses and the nights drew in. Revd. Tim and Elizabeth were snug in the vicarage after a diocesan grant for insulation had been awarded. They could now approach winter with confidence. Their LED bulbs helped to alleviate the coming darkness.

The arrival in the square of a police motorcycle was quite a novelty. PC Barnicoat carefully parked by the church wall and walked over to speak to Tim.

"I reckon you're the right man to speak to here in Goonperran. I'm not being funny, but a large black feline has been seen in the area. I don't mean a domestic cat," glancing over at Crowley who had set out to cross the square and see what was going on.

"No kidding, there's an escaped puma or something even larger that could have escaped from somewhere. It's dangerous and must not be approached.

"I'm off to warn the other parishes now. We don't expect it to approach the villages but, with winter coming, it might get desperate. I know that this sounds crazy, but please take it seriously."

Tim walked thoughtfully back to the vicarage. He was due to visit George Uren on his farm later and would ask him what he thought about it.

It appears that George thought quite a lot about it and had a fair amount to say.

"Come into the linhay and I'll show ''ee what 'tis about," he said grimly. In the dusty covered yard, he pulled back a bloody tarpaulin to show him the bodies of three sheep that had been ripped apart. Long scratches showed through the close wool of their flanks. Their throats had not been ripped out. Each had been killed by a deep bite in the back of the neck.

"No dog could have done this! 'Tis some sort of big cat. These sheep are here to be taken away and examined by DEFRA."

Driving back to Goonperran Tim hunched over the Land Rover's heater. The sky hung low and was slate grey. The wind blew from the east. Suddenly something large and black jumped down the hedge in front of Tim's vehicle. He jammed on the brakes and skidded hard. The creature flashed across the lane and leapt up and over the hedge on the other side.

Tim caught a glimpse of a powerful black feline with a sheep dangling from its mouth. A flat head with small round ears, yellow eyes, and a thick neck was followed by a lithe body and a long tufted tail. Powerful back legs propelled the beast out of sight in a flash.

When Tim arrived home he described the huge cat to Elizabeth.

"I now know it's real because I've seen it. There's nothing mystical or psychic about it."

Next day, the North Cornwall Drag Hunt met in the square.

"They'm doing something useful for a change," remarked Mrs Williams for the post office.

The hounds circled around each other, whining and barking expectantly. They were called to order by the whippers-in. The Master of the Hunt blew a blast from his short horn and the hunt clattered off. There were horses and ponies of all colours and sizes and men and women in dark blue jackets rising in the saddle as the hunt trotted away towards the moor.

They spent a happy day poking around thickets and following scents until three of the hounds went missing. They were eventually found in a terrible state; two were dead, the other so badly injured that the Master had to shoot it. All were covered in deep claw marks and bites. The hunt returned despondently to Goonperran after a fruitless day. The only thing they had to show for it was further proof of the beast's existence.

Next day, Tim answered the phone once again: "Hello, Vicar? 'Tis Sarah here. You know me as the White Witch. I can help you get rid of this beasty thing if you like. It seems to be a menace. None of us be safe. Can I come round and explain what I'd like to do?"

"Certainly, Sarah. The door's always open."

So Sarah came bustling around. She didn't look like a witch at all. She was quite young with long blond hair and a pleasant expression. She worked part-time at the Witchcraft Museum at Boscastle Harbour a little way up the coast.

Tim gave her a mug of tea.

"What do you propose to do to get rid of this awful creature? I have seen it. It's real and in no way paranormal. It would be difficult to shoot and dangerous to capture. It is doing a lot of damage round here and frightening everybody half to death."

"I just want to move it on, perhaps over the border to Dartmoor. So I'll call up the Wild Hunt to chase it away, not to kill it, but to show it that it's met its match."

"What on earth is the Wild Hunt, Sarah? Does it have anything to do with the Devil? We can't have that, you know!"

"There's nothing evil about the Wild Hunt. Not if it's properly controlled. It can be a force for good. As you know I've taken an oath to never do evil, that's why I've come to see you today."

Tim scratched his head. Should he be agreeing to this mad scheme? Would he be accused of being in league with occult forces? Would the Wild Hunt actually be of any help? Did it even exist?

"Oh, it exists alright and has done so for hundreds of years."

Tim realised that Sarah had just read his mind.

"The reason I've come to see you is to get your blessing. I could do it all on my own. We'm not in opposition, you know."

"Alright, please summon up the Wild Hunt and chase the beast all the way to England. I'll pray for success and for good to prevail."

"Thank you, Vicar. Just don't be surprised by what you hear and see soon. Unlike the Drag Hunt, it only operates at night. Don't be tempted to follow it too close. If you do so, it will take offence and vanish."

Tim was left pondering the implications of this ancient folk memory coming to life. He was learning to listen to the opinions of others, but wasn't this an extreme case?

He told Elizabeth about it and swore her to secrecy. He certainly didn't want the archdeacon and the bishop to hear about it. But, after thinking and praying for a long time he reckoned that a bit of give and take would hurt no one.

A couple of nights later a storm blew out of the west. Wind-blasted trees bent further and the last, clinging leaves were sent flying far into the dark sky. The moon shone fitfully, often obscured by a rack of scudding dark clouds. Rain spattered down like shrapnel; the wind boomed in a hollow sky.

Around midnight Tim and Elizabeth heard the ringing of horses' hooves on the road surface outside their bedroom window. They pulled back the curtain to see a melee of dark figures circling the square. The hounds were all black, with glowing red eyes. The horses were black, as were the jackets of the men who rode them. There was no baying from the hounds and no noise at all apart from the ringing of steel on stone.

Then the Master's horn sounded once. It was a high, antique sound quite unlike anything that Tim and Elizabeth had heard before. The master glanced up briefly at the window, as if seeking approval. His face was dead white with red eyes like the hounds.

Then they were off, clattering up towards the moor. Soon there was no trace left of them. The square fell silent as if they had never clustered there.

An hour later they were back, silent except for the sound of galloping steel-shod horses' hooves. Once more Tim and Elizabeth pulled back the curtain. In front of the hunt, a huge black feline loped frantically along, just keeping ahead of the hunt. As he rode by, the Master turned his white face once more to the window and tipped his cap with his riding crop. His eyes were silvered by the moon as it emerged briefly from dark clouds.

"I know where they're going," said Tim to Elizabeth. "We won't see hide nor hair of the beast again, you mark my words."

Next day, Sarah came back to the vicarage through the drizzle. The storm had blown itself out and the day was still and damp.

"Well Vicar, us've seen the last of 'ee. I watched as the beast ran towards the coast. By the time it got to Penjawler Cliff it was knackered. It had nowhere to turn, and it went over the cliff to be dashed to pieces on the rocks. The tide was coming in and took'n out with it halfway to Ireland. Us'll see no more of 'n, thank God."

"I'm glad you said that and thanked God. It shows we're on the same side. Thank you for what you have done. Most people will never know what happened and I think you'll agree that we must keep it that way." So ended, for the time being, the holy alliance between Revd. Tim and the White Witch.

Elemental

After the success of the conversion of George Pumphrey's cottage to a church-owned affordable rental property, the movement of the affordable homes spread in the North Cornish village of Goonperran. A long-abandoned market garden near the centre of the village was bought, and a number of affordable houses were planned. They were to be built around a green to have large back gardens for the growing of vegetables and the keeping of fowls. There was to be a community pond and play equipment for children.

Revd. Tim and his wife Elizabeth were delighted when the Parish Council gave the scheme their blessing. The land, a brownfield site that would not extend the village boundary, had been generously given by the owner, George Uren. He did not generally want it known that he had done so. He and his wife had no children or dependents and valued the future of the village more than their personal fortunes.

Tim took the trouble to walk over to the building site most days to see how it was getting on. He was pleased to see that the rich topsoil had been put in a mound at the side rather than being taken away and sold. It would be put back into the gardens of the houses when they were completed. There were five houses in a crescent shape, rising from the ground with traditional materials. Dry stone walls surrounded the project and a small community orchard was ready for planting. Because George's market garden had once been part of his farm, it had been given the name 'Hendra', Cornish for 'The Old Farm'.

There was a single Portacabin being used as the site office. Tim knocked on the door one chilly autumn morning.

"'Ow be? Any problems?"

The site manager looked up from the plans.

"Hi, Tim. I was going to phone you today. We have come across a problem, which could hold us up for a considerable time."

"I did wonder, seeing as no one seems to be on-site and working today. What is it?"

"We've found human remains. We're waiting for the police to turn up and examine them. If they're recent, we have a major problem, if historic, less so. The forensics people will be able to determine which they are."

As he spoke a police car and a transit van pulled up at the entrance to the estate. Tim and Al, the site manager, went down to meet them. Al had asked Tim to look at the remains as an interested party.

Led by a sergeant the three police officers and the forensic team followed the two men over to the back of the site where the community orchard was planned to be planted. A builder was waiting leaning on his Cornish spade. He spoke first: "I was digging some pits to see where the subsoil began when I noticed something white about three feet down. I then turned archaeologist and carefully dug round what you see here."

Tim gasped in surprise. He had seen plenty of human remains, whole and fragmentary, fresh and decayed, but never anything like this. Sprawling at the bottom of the trench was the skeleton of what must once have been a huge man. Massive leg bones joined the pelvis and the huge spread of the rib cage and the massive arms were surmounted by a relatively small skull. The jaw hung down showing rows of worn yellow teeth.

"He's enormous. Must be nine feet tall. Yet his head is out of proportion to the rest of his body. Let's give the forensic people a chance to date him."

Tim and Al went back to the site hut for a cup of tea while the forensics team, now dressed in paper suits with hoods, measured and examined the giant bones. It didn't take them long to decide that the bones were historic and that an archaeology team should be summoned. The area where the bones were found was taped off and permission for building work on the houses was given.

"Thank heavens for that," Al remarked. "I'll call the builders back to work straight away. They'll be glad not to lose a day's pay."

Tim told Elizabeth about the bones that evening.

"I wonder if they're Viking," she said. "This close to the coast and with them not being buried with the head to the west of the feet probably means that it wasn't a Christian burial."

"Hopefully the archaeologists will find some artefacts in the grave that will enable them to date him. What is strange, apart from his overall size, is his small head."

The archaeologists from Kernow Archaeology in Truro were keen and quick. They photographed everything and gently lifted the bones, minutely examining the soil underneath the body. They found a few pins, a knife, and a gold brooch. It was enough to establish that the body was from the Viking era and was Scandinavian. The bones would be kept for further examination and conservation at Truro Museum. Tim wondered if this was the right thing to do but kept quiet for the time being. His fears were not to prove groundless...

On Monday morning, Tim received a phone call:

"Hello, Vicar. Mrs Hoskins here. I live right beside the building site for affordable homes. Last night I heard someone running around inside the security fence throwing things around and laughing. I've reported it to the police and they're coming to take a look. I was quite alarmed. There were strange lights in the sky that I can't explain. That's why I'm telling you about it.

"The person causing the ruckus was very tall with a small head, very odd to look at. I do hope he won't be back tonight. My Arthur has a dicky heart and I'm worried about him."

"I'll see what can be done about this. Most likely it's some youth from outside the parish having a laugh at our expense. A few pints too many at the Carlyon Arms most likely."

Tim called in at the Carlyon Arms to see if anyone answering Mrs Hoskins' description had been in the pub last night.

"No, Tim, nobody of that description. You know I won't allow drunkenness in here. I could lose my licence. I would certainly have noticed an unusually tall man with the low ceilings in here."

Tim walked onto the building site. He found the builders tidying up the mess of timber and building materials and salvaging anything usable.

"Bleddy nuisance," said the Foreman. "Us knows that there is always opposition from a few rich outsiders to schemes like this, but I've not heard of any complaints in this parish. I can't fathom it out."

"Odd as Dick's hatband," Tim replied. Then he thought that he should consult Florence Pelleymounter, who might hold some of the answers.

Once again sitting in her warm kitchen in front of the Aga Tim explained the situation. Florence shook her head and replied:

"It sounds as if we have here an elemental. They are strange half-formed creatures, not quite human and of very low intelligence. They are rare, but they are dangerous. They move at high speed and wave their long arms in the air. The only features to be seen on their small heads are their eyes which show little sign of intelligence. They've never been photographed. All we have are drawings of them made after a sighting. They are very much a child's version of the human form."

"What on earth can we do about this one? He's disturbing the neighbours and, before long, he'll break out of the site security fence and charge around the village looking for trouble."

"He isn't a demon or a ghost. He's inchoate and half-formed. And not very clever although totally destructive. He can't be delivered or exorcised. There must be some way to lay him to rest."

"I have a few ideas, but I must talk to the archaeologists first."

That afternoon Tim took time to drive to Truro to talk to Kernow Archaeology in Truro Museum. In an office at the back of the building, Tim was welcomed by Dr Bates, the man in charge. Tim explained the situation, feeling a little foolish in front of a man of science. The reply did not surprise him:

"In all conscience, I can't release the bones yet. We still have quite a lot of work to do on them. I appreciate your predicament although I cannot altogether believe it. I don't actually see a clash between religion and science, but this is a very grey area for both of us. Give us a few days if you can. One question, though. Where will you bury the bones when you get them back to Goonperran? Our man was not a Christian, so a Christian burial in the holy ground is going to make the problem worse."

"Good point," said Tim. "I'll consult my Friend Dr Pelleymounter about it."

Tim drove home in the gathering dark, the draft whistling through the torn and ill-fitting canvas of his Land Rover. The heater clattered and struggled to keep producing heat. It finally gave up as Tim coasted down the long hill into Goonperran.

He was aware of a galloping sound beside the vehicle. He looked and nearly swerved into the hedge when he saw a tall figure running along beside him, waving its arms in the air. Its small head bobbed on its shoulders, a malevolent light shining from eyes as big as saucers. As it bobbed up and down it kept trying to reach into the Land Rover.

Tim put his foot down and shot round the final corner into the village. A high mewing sound followed him, and he crossed himself for protection. He managed to lose the creature and jumped out, over the wall, into the vicarage.

Florence was visiting Elizabeth when Tim came in, a wild look in his eyes.

"Don't tell me. You've seen the bugger. It chased you down the hill, didn't it? It seems that these things are so predictable. I'd hate to meet an intelligent elemental.

"I think we have a solution. When the science boys have finished with our Viking, we should bury him right back in the orchards he came from. I have a friend, Dr Olaf Pedersen. He's Norwegian and a bit of a pagan. He used to teach in my department before he retired after a long and distinguished career. I can contact him through the Witchcraft Museum, where he does a lot of voluntary work. I'm sure he will help us."

Dr Pedersen was contacted and was delighted to help. In the meantime, the elemental rampaged around the edges of the village, threatening, but doing no harm.

At last Dr Bates released the bones. They arrived in an unmarked van and were taken straight onto the building site. Dr Pedersen, Florence, Tim, Elizabeth, and the entire crew of builders assembled, hard hats in hand, to commit the bones back into the ground.

Tim and the assembled crowd understood very little of what Dr Pedersen intoned. They recognised the names of a few Norse gods, but the rest was unintelligible. They all cast handfuls of earth onto the bones before the builders, hurriedly but thoroughly, filled up the grave.

Dr Pedersen then produced a stone carved with runes, which was erected over the grave.

"What does it say," Tim asked.

"Here lies an unknown Viking, far from his native land but among apple trees. May his spirit cease from wandering and rest forever in the Halls of Valhalla."

"Thank you," said Tim, thinking: 'Different strokes for different folks.'

He heard from Dr Bates a few days later:

"I hope your problem is sorted. I have good news for you. The gold broach we found is, of course, a treasure trove. But half the value will go to the owners of the land on which it was found. The British Museum are keen to buy it. You could end up with a five-figure sum to go towards your excellent building project."

"Praise be!" Tim exclaimed!

Old Soldiers

To Revd. Tim and Elizabeth in Goonperran on 1 November always marked the beginning of winter and the turning point of the year. It was true that there would be calm, sunny days, even some warmth in the sun. But it was the damp and the low light levels that were hard to live with during the winter months.

With early November came Remembrance Day, the closest Sunday to 11 November, Armistice Day. Goonperran made a big thing of Remembrance. There were nine names of the fallen on the War Memorial below the church wall near the lych-gate. Tim compared the number of soldiers, sailors and airmen on the village Roll of Honour with the number who never came back. He knew that the average number of men killed in the British Army during the Great War was just under 10% of those who served. Goonperran had fed over 15% into the meat grinder. All the names were now on the granite War Memorial plaque.

Remembrance was the one occasion that Tim wore his old army beret and his three campaign medals, in honour of the fallen. He organised a bugler from his old regiment to play the Last Post and Reveille after the two-minute silence. He read the names of the fallen in a loud firm voice. The National Anthem and a hymn were sung before the people, or at least some of them, processed through the lych-gate into church for the late evening service.

There were usually over a hundred people gathered in front of the War Memorial for the short ceremony. The tricky bit was getting the church clock to strike eleven at exactly the right time after the silence. Sometimes, when the clock was behaving erratically, Tim asked one of the churchwardens to swing the bell eleven times. No one ever found out that it hadn't been the clock.

This November was unseasonably warm and still, so Tim decided on a candle-lit Remembrance ceremony. The Parochial Church Council enthusiastically backed him up and so it was on. The silence would be terminated by the clock striking nine, a fitting number because of the nine men who were killed in the Great War.

At just after eight-thirty Tim and Elizabeth handed out candles in jam jars to the assembling crowd. The choir were all present in their cassocks and surplices. The curate was dressed in a black cassock, cotta and stole, and Florence, the trainee lay reader, wore the same kit minus the stole.

Tim asked any descendants or relatives of the fallen to place their candles at the base of the memorial before going into church. Quite a few people wore their fathers' or grandfathers' medals on the right side of their jackets. A few wore them on the left side because they were veterans and had been there.

Tim read the names in his best parade ground voice, a form of address that Elizabeth and the people of Goonperran weren't used to. Then the two-minute silence began. Heads were bowed and the evening was still. The sun had gone down and there was a faint moon glow.

Everybody heard the vehicle approaching the square. There was the growling of an unfamiliar engine and the crash of gears. It sounded like nothing that anyone had heard before. Tim hoped it would see the assembled company and stop before it reached the square. With a roar, the vehicle pulled in by the churchyard wall under the trees and the engine stopped with a rumble.

Tim looked up to see a vehicle that was both familiar and strange at the same time. He identified it as a B Type Bus, used by London Transport before and during the Great War. By the faint lights around the square, Tim could see that it was roughly painted khaki. The windows of both the lower and upper decks were planked out and the words 'London Transport' were replaced by the letters 'WD', a broad arrow and a number. A circular open staircase led from the bottom to the top deck at the rear of the vehicle.

Tim was surprised that someone would have turned up at the ceremony unannounced and also late. He took a dim view of that. He looked for the driver and spotted him in the open cab. He was a small man wearing a bowler hat and a long dust coat. Perhaps Tim would have a quiet word with him later.

Then the tramp of feet was heard coming from the lane leading to the square. Nine men in uniform swung into the square, and their puttees immaculate, caps at the right angle, buttons shining and rifles at port arms. They crashed to a halt and grounded arms with no word of command.

Sparks flew from the hobnails and steel heel plates on their shining boots.

Although Tim was impressed, he felt that he should have been told that this tableau vivant was going to happen. Then something very strange happened.

The smart soldiers at the edge of the square moved forward in a shambling motion. Their puttees began to unravel, their uniforms became torn and filthy with mud and blood. A couple of the men dropped their rifles, staggering sideways. Bandages appeared on heads and round limbs. One man's ripped tunic fell open revealing the white shine of ribs and dark blood.

Men helped each other towards the bus. Those with limbs that were twisted were supported by bandaged men who could walk more easily. One by one, they were helped up into the bus by the driver in the long coat. Some slipped on the road surface and were caught by their comrades.

When the last man was safely on board the driver climbed back into his cab after turning the long handle below the square radiator twice to start the engine. It roared into life and the exhaust burbled.

Then, with a crash of gears, they were off, rumbling out of the square with the solid tyres slipping as the bus turned. It roared away towards the hill leading out of the village. After it had turned the corner, there was silence, broken only by the church clock striking nine o'clock in the high tower as the moon rose.

Tim continued as if nothing had happened. He reckoned that if you had to blag it then you had to blag it properly. He still didn't know who had organised the re-enactment and certainly intended to find out.

The service went well after the bugler performed flawlessly. After the service, many people congratulated Tim on the bus and the soldiers.

"One of they soldiers was the spitting image of my grandfather. I have his photo at home," said George Uren.

"That was quite a surprise, very effective," said Mrs Williams.

Florence Pelleymounter took a different view:

"Tim, I think we experienced a visitation from the dead. They were giving us their approval and showing us how it really was for them. They won't be back and there's nothing to worry about.

"They were reminding us that war is horrible, dirty, and bloody. There's no glory in it, only loss. We were privileged this evening to be shown a true vision."

"I know exactly what you're saying, Florence. It was too realistic to be a re-enactment, and the looks on the soldiers' faces were too familiar. No actors could have done that."

Despite what had happened Tim experienced no flashbacks to Iran or Afghanistan. He slept well in the knowledge that he had honoured the fallen of Goonperran in a true and sincere way.

The Second Augusta Legion

Late autumn in Goonperran brought its joys as well as its sorrows. Shortening days and later dawns were countered by coming home, pulling shut the curtains, and lighting the fire or firing up the log burner with well-seasoned ash, beech or oak. Early nights and sound sleep made life easier for everyone.

Revd. Tim was not a great television watcher, nor was Elizabeth. But they did enjoy archaeology programmes, particularly when the digs were not too far from home. They were most interested to discover that a Roman fort had been discovered at Roche. The familiar layout of an enclosing rectangle with rounded corners, the foundations of barrack blocks and stables and admin. buildings showed that the Romans had indeed been in Cornwall. The reason was obvious, they were searching for tin.

The finding of coins of the Emperor Vespasian and the masons' marks from the Second Augusta Legion all made sense. There were even villas being discovered in Cornwall; wonders never ceased. Perhaps rich Romans had taken advantage of their wealth to have second homes in a beautiful and generally mild part of their far-flung empire. Tim thought wryly that great wealth had always resulted in privilege at the expense of those who struggled to make a living.

Elizabeth was organising a module at school on the Roman occupation of Britain. It was multi-media, involving model making, lots of research, dressing up as Romans, cooking Roman food, and generally examining how the Romans lived. It dealt with the plusses of good roads, laws that worked, technical progress and the minuses of imperialism, slavery and human greed.

The children in the top two years of the school took enthusiastically to the project. They even produced a few Roman coins, not found locally, but bought in car boot sales, or found up country. Elizabeth had an academic from the University of Penwith come to the school to identify coins and some artefacts.

There was one artefact in particular that caught Dr Billings' eye. It had been found locally by the daughter of a local farmer over towards Trejago.

"What do you think it is?" asked Dr Billings.

"I think it's part of a roof tile," replied Loveday Goss. "Can you see the dog's paw print on it?"

"You're absolutely right! It's part of the flat part of the roof tile, called the tegula. It must have been made on a warm day and set out to dry in the sun. While it was drying a dog wandered over it leaving his paw print. This happened nearly two thousand years ago."

Before Dr Billings left for points west, he had a word with Elizabeth.

"May I have a word with Loveday, please? Her find is exceptionally interesting. I'd like to give her my card and write a note to her parents. We could have another significant Roman site here in Cornwall."

When the coins and other Roman bits and bobs had been put away Dr Billings asked Loveday exactly where she found the piece of tile.

"It was out in Furze Quartils, years ago. My dad said I must keep it because it could be important. I'm sure he'd like to talk to you about it."

And so it came about that Dr Billings drove up to the farm a few days later to meet Joseph Goss, farmer and member of the Methodist Church. The two men got on well and Joseph agreed to have a survey done on the field in question.

Tim happened to be visiting at the time and was happy to be included in the research. Money was found for a geophysical survey and a few weeks later a man with a strange machine like a mechanised wheelbarrow spent hours trundling across Furze Quartils. Unfortunately, the results were inconclusive because of the presence of so much shillet and mineral deposits. However, one rounded corner of the foundations of a wall was found. The evidence was enough to warrant a dig.

In early December, archaeology students in waterproofs started to dig three trenches. After several windy and soggy days, all they had found was a recent horseshoe, a Victorian penny, and Wood's Areca Nut Toothpaste jar lid, nothing Roman at all.

Sitting in the tent one dark evening Dr Billings gathered his sodden team about him.

"I'm afraid we're going to have to call it a day. We'll get no further funds unless we find some Roman finds. Loveday's tile might have been an anomaly, a piece of Roman tile from somewhere else caught up in a pile of earth or rubble and dumped years ago in the field. Tomorrow will have to be the last day on the dig, I'm afraid. It was a useful training exercise, anyhow."

Next day's dig yielded precisely nothing, so trenches were filled in and the site was left immaculate. The team said goodbye to Joseph Goss and left to go back west.

That evening Tim had a phone call:

"Hello, Revd. Tim, this is Loveday. The archaeology team have left the farm, but I think they've made a mistake. I've seen Roman soldiers in the next field. I've also heard them. They look at me as they march past as if they recognise me, yet they look puzzled."

"Loveday, that's most interesting. Do you think I could have a word with your dad?"

"Of course, he's seen them too. But he didn't say anything to Dr Billings because scientists need evidence. That's what Mrs Tremaine tells us at school."

"Quite right too. Oh, hello Joseph. What time of day did you see these Romans?"

"Hello, Tim. Thanks for taking us seriously. We see them in the early evening in the dimpsey. They are very clear and we hear them marching too."

"May I come out this evening? They probably won't appear if they know we're looking for them, but we must give it a try."

"Certainly, Tim. Look forward to seeing you."

Tim and Elizabeth drove a couple of miles out to the farm. It was well-kept and tidy, showing pride in the place that wasn't always common. They parked the Land Rover in the yard by the barn and knocked on the farmhouse door.

Joseph Goss came out, putting on his waxed jacket.

"Us'll have a look for a while and then a cup of tea in the kitchen to warm us up."

Joseph and his daughter, Tim and Elizabeth walked out to the field beside Furze Quartils. Joseph explained that it was called Arethornes and was used for grazing his small herd of milking cows. They waited by the gate under the cover of the hedge. And they waited quite a long time.

Just as they were thinking of going, a faint tramp of feet was heard from the other end of the field. By this time the moon was up. Then misty figures appeared four abreast and the sound of a ram's horn was heard.

Tim could not believe his eyes. A column of dirty, ragged Roman soldiers was advancing toward them across the field. They seemed to be cut off at the ankle. Their helmets were dull and dented, their dark red tunics stained, and their shields battered. They marched in step, but they seemed desperately tired. The Centurion who led them limped a little from a cut on his leg. The standard bearer followed with the eagle held aloft. It was missing one of its wings.

Behind the marching men were other soldiers carrying still forms on stretchers. Their short swords were sheathed. Behind them was a small rabble of women and children.

The Century was now only a few yards from Tim and the waiting group. The Centurion turned slightly and lifted a hand to Tim before moving on. Gradually the marching men began to fade away as the moon rose on an empty field.

Tim and the others made their way quietly to the farmhouse. Sitting around the table, each told what he or she had seen. The stories all tallied.

"Right," said Tim. "Tomorrow I'll phone Dr Billings. I won't tell him what we saw but will say that some new evidence has turned up in Arethornes. I think that the Century was marching down the main street of the fort after a skirmish. They were heading outside the wall to bury their dead. I'll ask Dr B to bring the geophys team for just one day."

"Great idea! I would love them to find something conclusive on my farm. I'm not just interested in farming, you know."

Tim got his way. Dr Billings never did ask what the additional evidence had been. He didn't have to. Geophysics revealed that the route taken by the Century was indeed the main street of the fort. When a trench was dug at the site of the south gate, a lintel stone with grooves from the iron rims of chariot wheels was found. Farther on some burials were excavated. Many of the bones showed cut marks and breaks, injuries received in battle.

Even better was the masons' mark of the Second Augusta Legion on the foundation stone of the gatehouse. Coins from that era were also found and a long occupation was proved.

One evening, Tim and Elizabeth relaxed in from of their log burner.

"Tim, those Roman soldiers knew we were there. They were aware of our presence. One or two perked up when they saw me, straightened their backs and their spears and marched a little more smartly despite their fatigue and their wounds."

"Yes. I know that they wanted us to see them and find the fort. Now their job is done, and they are laid to rest."

Delilah

About once a week Revd. Tim and Elizabeth went to the Carlyon Arms in the evening to relax and also to talk to people they didn't normally see. They enjoyed their snug pints under beams and low ceilings.

One Friday in early December, Tim and Elizabeth sat on an old settle near the fire listening to the music on the jukebox. The landlord had the sense to keep the volume down so that people didn't have to shout to make themselves heard.

Tim was feeling particularly tired after too many meetings during the week. He'd chaired most of them and had to delicately turn some people away from witterings and repetition. It left him drained, and he was enjoying his evening after tea in the pub.

Then a familiar song came onto the juke box and Tim couldn't help but prick up his ears like a tired hound finally picking up the scent of a fox. It was 'Delilah', sung by Tom Jones.

"O, o, o, Delilah..." The melody was catching, but the meaning was dark. It concerned a man who had just stabbed his lover to death and was waiting for the police to come and break down the door and arrest him.

"You know, Liz, this song always makes me feel really angry and I don't know why."

"Really? That's unlike you, Tim. Perhaps you need a holiday."

"No chance of that at the moment..."

The music finished, but the joy had gone out of the evening. The song had made Tim think. He knew what it was like to stab someone. In Iraq, he had bayoneted a terrorist who was coming at him with a machete. He would normally have shot the man, but he was in the middle of changing magazines on his SA 80. He did it without thinking, a totally instinctive act of violence that he had been trained to do. It had doubtless saved his life. He found the congratulations of his soldiers hard to bear. It made him feel sick.

How could he share this with his wife? Never mind, an early night would take care of the matter.

Next day, he dragged himself out of bed and over to St Piran's Church where he prayed for guidance. He knew he had to talk to Elizabeth and explain what was happening to him. Was he becoming a victim of repressed PTSD?

He lost himself in his work, caring for the parish and helping his fellow man. The day passed quickly, and he felt more relaxed when he returned home in the evening. Elizabeth was making pasties for tea and singing quietly to herself.

"O, O, O, Delilah; O, O, O, Delilah..."

Tim tensed up as a surge of anger rose in him, making him feel dizzy. He picked up a sharp knife and was about to shout when he caught himself and put it down. He sat down shaking all over.

"Oh, Tim, I'm so sorry. I forgot you hated that song. It's a real earworm. I just can't get it out of my head."

"I don't know what came over me; some sort of flashback, I think. You know I love you more than anything in the world."

And could never hurt you. He continued thinking. But he wasn't so sure of that. After all, he had grabbed the knife and nearly plunged it into Elizabeth's chest. It would have been easy. And then all those terrible feelings would have gone away. It was all too terrible to contemplate.

"Liz, tomorrow I'm going to the doctor's for a referral for PTSD. I want to be cured of these feelings of anger. They have nothing to do with you, I promise. You must trust me on this."

"Of course, Tim. The things you have seen are bound to have an effect, even years later. I do understand. And you do know that I love you."

So Tim drove to Bodmin to see Dr Couch. He told him what had happened and asked to be referred to a PTSD specialist. This was granted and Tim had an appointment at Bodmin General Hospital. He took tests and answered questions ad nauseam. He kept his patience but mentioned the trigger of the song that caused him such distress and anger. The doctor asked him if he had heard that particular song in Iraq or Afghanistan and Tim replied that he had not. Now he had to wait for the test results to come back from analysis.

A few days later, Tim had a phone call from the hospital arranging a follow-up session. He duly arrived and was ushered into the office of the senior consultant.

"Revd. Tremaine, I'm not sure if the news is good or bad. You have absolutely no trace of PTSD. You seem to have dealt with past traumas in an admirable way. I'm sure that your religious faith must have helped. Your stable character is also on your side.

"This brings us to why you have these episodes. We know what the trigger is, but what we don't know is why. This concerns me. Do you have any marital problems?"

Tim replied that he did not. He cared for his wife more than he did for himself. He would pray and meditate and find a way out of this irrational anger. He thanked the doctor and went away mystified.

When he arrived home he had an idea. He would talk to Florence Pelleymounter early the next day and then explain the conclusion to Elizabeth.

He found time to go to Florence's house and sat, once more, in her warm kitchen full of friendly cats and spices warmed by the enormous Aga. He explained the situation to her and then sat back to listen to what she said:

"Tim, I think I know what is wrong. The Devil is still roaming around seeing whom he can destroy. You seem to be near the top of his list! You are a priest, and a very good one. If he can bring you down, he'll also bring down many members of your congregations in four parishes. He'll drag the dear old Church of England into the mire.

"I've always heard that the Devil targets those nearest God's altar. This is one more example of that. Awareness of a problem is the first step to solving it. We can overcome this problem with prayer. Now you must talk to Elizabeth. This will help more than anything to solve the problem."

Tim thanked Florence and went home with love and resolve in his heart.

"Liz, you must understand that what I am about to tell you is in no way your fault..." He explained it all, and they prayed together.

Life returned to normal over the next few days. Then Friday evening arrived. The couple went off to the Carlyon Arms as usual anticipating a quiet and relaxing evening. They sat down in their usual seats and listened to the jukebox playing in the corner.

Then a familiar and haunting song made its presence felt. It was, of course, Tom Jones singing 'O, O, O, Delilah'. Tim tensed, then relaxed again. He grabbed Elizabeth and kissed her. A few cheers rose from the room and a few people clapped.

"That's how I feel about you, Liz. What God has ordained may no man put asunder."

"Or the Devil," added Elizabeth, blushing to the roots of her dark hair.

When they returned home they sat down and Elizabeth said: "Some people are affected by certain passages of music. Have you ever heard Billie Holliday sing 'Gloomy Sunday'? It's all about suicide and is known as the 'Hungarian Suicide Song' because it was composed by a Hungarian composer who did, actually take his own life. It was banned for years on the BBC and other radio channels because they thought it encouraged some people to take their own lives."

"I have heard it, actually, but it had no effect on me. I really think now, God willing, our musical troubles are behind us."

Rats, Rats, as Big as Bloomin' Cats

Winter settled on Goonperran like a shroud. Christmas was approaching and Revd. Tim was very busy arranging special services for all four parishes in his care. His army organisational skills were used to their fullest in balancing the needs of each parish against the needs of all the others. There was great satisfaction in getting it right and horrible frustration in double booking.

Rumours of the appearance of a beast on the moor were circulating once more. Tim hoped it wasn't the creature he had dealt with back in the autumn. He was soon to find that it wasn't.

"Gurt humpy thing, big as a dog, with yellow teeth and a long tail," Sarah told him one day in the post office. Mrs Williams had, as usual, something to add:

"Nigel the Postman from St Austell saw it the other day. He said it looked like a giant rat. When he drove on, he saw several more of them."

"It seems we're always under attack," Tim said. "But with God's help we'll overcome this one." He carried on with his visiting and forgot all about giant rats and beasts on the moor.

A couple of nights later he turned over in bed wondering why a flock of sheep was being driven through the village in the middle of the night. The trouble was that they didn't sound quite like sheep. Their progress was more like a rustling sound, flowing through the village.

Next morning, there was no sign of any sheep or any other animals for that matter. Tim put on his cycling clothes. He was due to visit several parishioners in the next parish, Polcriddick. He opened the side door and took his bike by the handlebars. It responded sluggishly to his pushing, and he looked down. Both tyres and the saddle were missing. Shreds of rubber and leather hung from the wheel rims and the skeleton of the saddle. Was this a joke? Tim didn't think so.

Turning the corner of the house towards the front gate Tim stopped in amazement. There, in front of him, was the corpse of the biggest rat he had ever seen. It lay on its side with shreds of rubber hanging from its open mouth from which two yellow teeth protruded. Its fur was dark and matted but white along the line of its bulging stomach. A long, bare, heavy tail curved away from its powerful hindquarters. It was the size of a large dog.

Tim took an old tarpaulin out of the shed and covered the body. It smelled of urine. He then went back into the house to warn Elizabeth not to lift the tarpaulin and explained what he had found. Before setting out to drive to Polcriddick, he phoned David George the DEFRA man, explaining what he has seen and what he had done with the body.

"You've done the right thing. There is a high risk of Weil's disease and other nasties. I'll be over as soon as I can with a van. See you at around midday."

So Tim did his rounds in the next parish and returned home to find David George sitting in his van outside the vicarage.

"Have you been here long, David?"

"No, five minutes or so. It gave me the chance to look up 'super rats'. This creature couldn't have been a capybara because they are entirely vegetarian. Let's have a look at our departed friend."

Tim took him round the corner to find that the tarpaulin was lying flat on the path. Whatever had been under it had vanished.

"Blow me down!" said Tim. "Good thing I took a few photos on my phone. I'm pretty sure it was dead. It wasn't breathing and had apparently choked to death on one of my bicycle tyres."

David had a careful look at the images on Tim's phone and then examined his bike.

"Yes, the bite marks in the alloy of the rims are definitely from a rat and an enormous one at that. But how it disappeared goodness knows. I'll do some research back at the office and be in touch."

Tim was puzzled as to how the dead rat could have disappeared. Surely nobody could have taken it for a joke. Elizabeth wouldn't have carried it away or buried it. Did he have a phantom rat on his hands?

His next visitor was PC Warren, the firearms officer.

"Hello, Tim. I'm here to check your pistol and your firearms certificate. I have to do it, even though you're a vicar."

"No problem Frank. You'll find everything in order. Come into the office. I'll show you the certificate and where I keep the pistol."

"Thank you, Tim, I appreciate it."

The certificate was in order and Tim handed Frank the pistol from a locked steel cupboard. Frank looked at it and put it on the table.

"We'll have a re-run of that," said Tim, handing the pistol back to Frank, who, getting the message, opened the weapon and checked that each of the cylinders was empty.

"That's better, Frank. We can't forget our range safety rules."

"Sorry, Tim. I know why you keep this revolver. An ex-soldier can never be off his guard. Smith and Webley service revolver. Old but effective. A good thing I won't ask you where you got it from."

"Touche. Have you got time for a cup of tea?"

Sitting in the kitchen he told Frank about the giant rat and its disappearance. Frank said he would keep his eyes open and took his leave.

The phone rang in its insistent tone.

"Hello, Tim here."

"It's David from DEFRA. Your rat is an impossibility, even if I saw the photos with my own eyes. There are super rats, but they don't grow as large as yours. There were packs of them between the wars on the Welsh borders. Even a case of bike tyres and saddles being eaten. Until we have a body as evidence we can't do anything. I have a feeling, however, that we haven't heard the last of this ratty story."

Whenever Tim took the Land Rover out, he made sure that he took the revolver with him in the glove compartment. He never knew when he would need it. One evening, as the sun was sinking into the sea, he drove back from Trejago. Coming round the corner he stepped hurriedly on the brake pedal as he saw a mass of huge grey furry bodies filling the lane from one stone hedge to another. Red eyes glared at him, dozens of them, daring him to drive on.

He did so, accelerating into the furry wall, feeling the crunch of bones and the release of entrails. He heard squeals of pain and rage and the scrabbling of claws on the road surface as the survivors leapt up the hedge banks. One of two of the rats took the offensive and tried to jump into the Land Rover. Tim shot three of them. The sharp bangs of the pistol and the stink of cordite stopped others in their tracks.

When all living rats had gone Tim stepped carefully out of the vehicle. The front was smeared with fur and blood. Dead rats lay twisted in the road, their entrails steaming in the cold air. Once again, Tim took photographs. He dragged the corpses to the sides of the lane and drove off with one dead rat thrown into the back of the Land Rover as evidence.

But, on arriving home, he wasn't surprised to find that the rat that had been sprawled in the back of his vehicle was no longer there. He turned round and drove back the way he had come to see if it had fallen out of the side of the Land

Rover. There was no sign of it or of any of the others at the massacre site. *What*, thought Tim, *was real?*

There was no blood, no fur, nothing. The battered front of the Land Rover was completely clean. Even the strong smell of urine was gone. How could DEFRA deal with phantom rats? His friend David would think he was losing his grip.

Still looking around in the road for something to convince Tim that what he had seen had actually happened, he found the flattened remains of three bullets lying on the road surface. He put them in his pocket as proof to himself that he had killed the rats.

The only person Tim ever told about that phantom rat pack was Elizabeth. She believed him and observed that nobody else should be told. They would listen out for any more rat stories over the next few weeks.

A few weeks later, Tim and Elizabeth were in the post office paying their subscription to the Church Times.

"Us hasn't seen hide nor hair of they bloomin' rats, praise be," Mrs Williams remarked.

"And a good thing too," replied Tim.

On the way home, Elizabeth suddenly said: "Take up arms against a sea of troubles and by opposing, end them."

"Which book of the Bible does that come from?"

"Shakespeare, silly. But you know that... don't you??"

A Plague on One of Your Parishes

With Christmas over and January beginning... its long drag Goonperran settled down to do what it was best at, enduring. Unfortunately, the parish didn't know what it was going to have to endure...

Revd. Tim and his wife Elizabeth were happy and snug in the vicarage. Thick granite walls and small windows shielded them from winter storms that rolled in waves from the Atlantic. Good insulation and a good roof helped too. So did a positive attitude and lots of hard work. But there was always a surprise in the offing...

One frosty night, Tim woke up very early with a deep feeling of unease. He leaned over to kiss Elizabeth and was horrified to find that she had no lips or nose. What he had so lovingly kissed was teeth and gristle. The hand he held briefly had only two fingers.

He quickly switched on the bedside lamp to find that his Elizabeth was sleeping soundly and was complete, with no parts missing. He must have had a waking dream that continued for a while. Saying a quick prayer for protection, not only from evil but also from his own imagination, he settled down to another hour's sleep, snug and warm.

When he got out of bed he remembered what he had experienced but said nothing about it to Elizabeth. She helped to make breakfast and then set off on the short walk to school for another day's teaching and administration. Tim went to open St Piran's Church and knelt at the altar rails to pray. He felt listless and rather unwell.

When Elizabeth came home, she complained of a headache and swollen glands. Tim made her a cup of tea and gave her a couple of paracetamols. He took two himself.

"I think we're coming down with something. It's most inconvenient."

"After I've prepared tomorrow's lessons I think I'll go to bed early. I want to fight off whatever bug I have."

"Good idea, Liz. I'll sleep in the spare room so as not to disturb you."

Next day, they both felt slightly better and went to work as usual. Tim had to go to the post office and Mrs Williams had this to say:

"The doctor's surgery was full this morning. Lots of people are complaining of sore patches on their skin and headaches. Dr Singh is trying to find out what it is that's exactly wrong with them. It's most unusual as well as distressing."

"I hope he gets to the bottom of this soon. We can't have an epidemic in this parish."

Elizabeth came home in the late afternoon reporting that many of her children were away sick. Two of the secretaries and one of the teachers had complained of sore skin patches as well. She was concerned that two places on the back of her hands were losing feeling.

Tim went to his laptop and typed in the symptoms he had heard were rampant in the village. He soon came up with the answer:

"Liz, you're not going to like this, but the answer seems to be leprosy."

"Really? Have you ever read 'Three Men in a Boat'? The author, who calls himself 'J', feels unwell and looks in a medical dictionary. He decides that he has everything mentioned there with the possible exception of housemaid's knee."

"Good point, Liz, but I think I'll talk to someone up at Bodmin General. It could do some good."

Next day, he drove his stinking Land Rover to Bodmin to talk to the consultant responsible for infectious diseases. Dr Chatterjee received him warmly, sitting him down in his office and sending for a welcome cup of tea.

"Tim, I know you wouldn't be talking to me here if the matter were not serious, so, out with it."

Tim explained that many of his parishioners were coming down with headaches, skin patches and areas of no feeling.

"It sounds like leprosy although the disease is very rare in this country and has been for quite some time. Let me see the back of your left hand."

The doctor examined a discoloured patch and then took a sterilised needle and pricked the area. Tim felt no pain, even when a drop of blood beaded on the back of his hand.

"How old are you, Tim?"

"Thirty-three last birthday."

"One can catch leprosy at any age, but a fit young man like you should not be showing symptoms so quickly. I'll take blood and urine samples, and let you know the results as quickly as I can.

"Leprosy is caused by contact with others who already have the disease. So don't go kissing anyone, especially not your wife. Avoid unnecessary human contact and don't alarm anyone. It may not be leprosy; in fact, I will be very surprised if it is."

On his drive back to Goonperran, Tim noticed a new archaeological dig just outside the village. In a field next to a stream overhung with trees, he saw an old friend, Dr Pengelly, from Kernow Archaeology. He stopped to say hello.

"Hello, Tom, what are you hoping to find here? It's quite a remote spot and far from any settlement."

"That's the point, Tim. Mediaeval people didn't build leper hospitals in the middle of villages you know. Come and see what we've found so far."

Tom Pengelly showed Tim a trench, which had uncovered the foundations of what appeared to be quite a large room.

"This is, we think, the infirmary. People with all sorts of skin diseases apart from leprosy would be sent here. The problem was that those who were cured could never be sent back into society. They were branded as lepers, and they remained lepers, even though they weren't."

"A bit draconian. Tell me, could any leprosy virus be transmitted from this site to anyone living nearby?"

"No chance whatsoever. The disease dies with the carrier, unlike cholera. If it were the case that leprosy could spread in this way, we wouldn't be allowed to dig here. We'd be the first to contract it and a lot of our business would fall off."

"Very funny, Tom! I'll be back from time to time to see what you and your team have found."

Within a few days, the leprosy symptoms faded and feeling came back to the affected skin patches. Tim and Elizabeth stopped worrying about each other and life in the parish returned to relative normality. Then Tim had a phone call from Tom the Archaeologist:

"Tim, we've found two more important pieces of evidence: the first is a few burials, and some of the bones show signs of leprosy, but the rest do not. These were the unfortunate souls who were condemned to live the rest of their lives in the leper hospital. The second find is much more unusual.

"We dug up a lead tablet with a curse scratched on it, like a Roman tablet. It reads: 'A curse of the people of Goonperran. May they have the leprosy that I have never had. May they rot for years until they die. May this curse prevail for as long as this lead should last. May they be as unhappy as I was all the years I was forced to live in this leper hospital. Eliza Polgrean 1567'."

Tim told Elizabeth about the finds and the curse. They prayed for the soul of Eliza Polgrean and for the health of the people of Goonperran.

Next day, the symptoms were back. Many people in the parish woke up with a feeling of dismay. Once again, the village surgery was besieged by lots of people with the same symptoms. Tim sought the help of his trainee lay reader Florence Pelleymounter.

"Well, Tim. Most people don't know about the curse, so it can't be working through auto-suggestion. It must be genuine, in which case we have a real problem on our hands. Innocent people are beginning to suffer for an attitude that their ancestors were not responsible for. Folk memories of the Black Death still existed in the Late Mediaeval and Early Modern eras.

"The solution is obvious but nearly impossible. The lead artefact must be destroyed. But how can a valuable piece of archaeological evidence be made to disappear? What academic would agree to have such an object melted down?"

"I can only ask," replied Tim, gloomily.

As the village became sicker Tim decided he had to act. He was about to phone Dr Pengelly when the phone rang.

"Hello, Tim, Tom here. I understand you're having a problem in the parish, a possibly psycho-somatic hysteria of leprosy. I don't know how anyone, but yourself could know about the curse. I'm sure you've told nobody about it.

"I'm pretty sure that the lead tablet is a fake. Indications of how some of the words are spelled and phrased show a much more modern provenance. After careful research, I think that only the Museum of Witchcraft in Boscastle would display it.

"With a clear conscience, I have had it photographed. I have also had a replica made with 'Replica' stamped on the back. I will stick my neck out by giving you the original and not asking what you will do with it."

"Thank you very much, Tom. You are doing the parish a great favour. I definitely owe you one."

Next day, Tom, feeling groggy and rather leprous, drove up to the archaeological site. Tom was there to greet him and show him around the greatly enlarged dig. Apart from the infirmary, they had found the foundations of a chapel and the dorter, where everyone slept. More burials had been uncovered, many of the finger and toe bones were missing, and there were holes in some of the long bones where lesions had occurred.

In the Portacabin that served as an office, Tom carefully handed Tim a heavy object wrapped in brown paper.

"I'm trusting you to tell nobody about this, ever. I'm risking my academic reputation by doing this. I love what I do. But, in all conscience, I cannot let your parish suffer."

"Thank you, Tom. I won't forget this. You're a good man."

"I hope God thinks so as well."

Tim was certain that He did. At the vicarage, he took the lead tablet, which he was sure did date from the sixteenth century, and put it in an empty tin can on the fire. He and Elizabeth watched as it bubbled and shrank, losing shape and form and all potency. He then took a pair of tongs and lifted the tin out of the flames. A tin-plated blob of lead lay in the bottom.

Tim took it outside and buried it deep beneath the lawn. Then he came back inside.

"Liz, show me the back of your hands, please."

She did so, and Tim was delighted to see that they were clear of any stain or blemish. He looked down at his own to find them in exactly the same condition.

As the days went by, people drifted back to work, and the surgery was almost empty. The school was back to normal, and everyone was happy that they felt better at last. They would never know what really had occurred.

Then the phone rang once more. It was the bishop's secretary. She made an appointment for him, to see the bishop on the following day. Tim was concerned that something had leaked out of Goonperran and reached the bishop's ear.

Next day, he drove down to Truro in his battered and toxic Land Rover, polluting the king's highway all the way down west. He was courteously ushered into the bishop's office. Bishop Gerald looked gravely at him.

"Tim, it's time we reviewed the first year and a half of your cure of souls in Goonperran, Trejago, and the other two parishes.

"Your tenure has been unconventional, to say the least. But, from all accounts, it has been very successful, and I must congratulate you. Your people love you and your lovely wife. Congregations are increasing in all four parishes and, miracle of miracles, they have all paid their parish shares. You have made the best use of your curate, and your lay reader is showing great promise.

"Now to the other matter. Through no fault of your own, you are a magnet for psychic disturbance and the paranormal. You have dealt with it extremely well. I'm very glad that I have appointed you Deliverance Minister. It seems to have confined the ghosties, ghoulies and long-legged beasties to your own parishes and kept the others clear. Undoubtedly, this will change in time.

"Now, to the matter of your evil-smelling and disreputable mode of transport. The Church of England has a very firm policy on climate change. Your old Land Rover has probably been responsible for the destruction of at least two glaciers and several huge icebergs. I propose to make available to you a grant to buy a decent second-hand four-by-four that will enhance your parish rather than pollute it. We have some funds at our disposal and feel that the time has come.

"And, by the way, we still need a rural dean. No money available for that, of course. What did you say, Tim? Is that bit of army slang really suitable for the ear of a bishop?"

Milton Keynes UK
Ingram Content Group UK Ltd.
UKHW020617281123
433366UK00014B/306